BEWITCHING THE EARL

LAUREN SMITH

Edited by Noah Chinn

Excerpt from *An Earl By Another Name* by Lauren Smith

Cover Art by Angela Haddon

ISBN: 978-1-947206-41-0 (e-book edition)

ISBN: 978-1-947206-42-7 (print edition)

OTHER TITLES BY LAUREN SMITH

Historical

The League of Rogues Series

Wicked Designs

His Wicked Seduction

Her Wicked Proposal

Wicked Rivals

Her Wicked Longing

His Wicked Secret (coming soon)

His Wicked Embrace (coming soon)

The Seduction Series

The Duelist's Seduction

The Rakehell's Seduction

The Rogue's Seduction

Standalone Stories

Tempted by A Rogue

Sins and Scandals

An Earl By Any Other Name

A Gentleman Never Surrenders

A Scottish Lord for Christmas

Contemporary

The Surrender Series

The Gilded Cuff

The Gilded Cage

The Gilded Chain

Her British Stepbrother

Forbidden: Her British Stepbrother

Seduction: Her British Stepbrother

Climax: Her British Stepbrother

Paranormal

Dark Seductions Series

The Shadows of Stormclyffe Hall

The Love Bites Series

The Bite of Winter

Brotherhood of the Blood Moon Series

Blood Moon on the Rise

Brothers of Ash and Fire

Grigori

Mikhail

Rurik

Sci-Fi Romance

Cyborg Genesis Series

Across the Stars (coming soon)

I

Strange, how one's future can hang upon a single moment. One can feel trapped, frozen, while the world spins wildly by. Daphne Westfall was caught in such a moment, unable to move forward now that her life had been turned upon its head. Ever since her father's death, she dwelt in a nightmare that had no visible end.

She shivered on the snowy sidewalk, hand extended toward passersby, praying someone would have mercy on her. They dodged her with lips curled in sneers of disgust. Another gust of wind blew in from the river and whipped her threadbare skirt about her legs. She stamped her feet and then pressed her legs tightly together, hoping to conserve warmth, but she still couldn't feel her toes. Her hands were dry and cracked, her once clean nails layered with the grime of the streets.

Tears stung her eyes. Just a few pennies before nightfall would keep her out of the White House Brothel in Soho. She bit her lip and mentally fled from that option. To go there would finally break her.

Her aching stomach rumbled. But she had to be pragmatic if she hoped to fill her aching stomach, warm her shivering body beside a fire and sleep in a warm bed.

Daphne resisted the urge to touch the secret pocket in her dress, where she'd hidden her mother's pearls. Another woman might have sold the pearls to eat, but Daphne couldn't bring herself to do it. The single, elegant strand was all she had left of her mother, the only thing the courts of England hadn't been able to pry from her fingertips as they carried her father to prison.

When her father had been convicted of counterfeiting, Sir Richard Westfall's estate had been seized by the Crown and his property sold to settle his debts to his victims. Daphne had been cast out into the cold with nothing but a single dress and her mother's pearls tucked away in a hidden pocket.

"Please—please, sir," she whispered to a passerby. "A few pennies..."

The man spat on her open, trembling palm. She shrank back with a wince and hastily wiped his spit off on her gown. More tears escaped as shame threatened to suffocate her.

Sell the pearls and you won't face this anymore... a dark voice whispered in her head. But she couldn't.

A man and a woman paused on the street a few feet away and stared. Hope surged. She knew that woman. Lady Esther Cornelius, a friend, once.

Esther stared hard at her, then whispered something to her companion who, although a good distance away, tossed a small pouch of coins. In the past, she would have hidden from a familiar face, ashamed to be seen in such a state, but right now all she could think about was her hunger. To her shame, she leapt at the pouch, landing hard in the icy puddle along the alley. She caught the pouch and clutched it to her chest. When she looked up, Lady Esther and her companion were walking away.

Daphne sniffed, her nose burning as she tried to keep her

tears at bay. How she wished she could curse her father. He loved her, just as she loved him, yet he had destroyed her life, her future...everything.

She wasn't sure how long she sat there, shivering and clutching the small pouch to her chest, before she tucked it safely in her skirts and glanced about. Her attention caught on the figure of a tall, handsome man leaning against the wall of a shop across the street. His exquisite clothes and refined appearance marked him for a gentleman.

Fear crawled up her spine. Why would a gentleman be watching a beggar woman? Perhaps he was not as gentlemanly as he appeared. Would he steal the coins, take her mother's pearls? She wouldn't let him. She pushed to her feet and hurried down the street, fighting the urge to run.

She glanced over her shoulder. He followed on the opposite side of the street. She quickened pace. The man suddenly vanished from view as a crowd of people swept past him. She stopped beside a row of coaches parked along the street close by and scanned the crowd.

"Miss Westfall." She started to turn toward that voice when strong fingers seized her arm.

Her shoulder collided with a hard chest. She cried out. The door of the nearest coach opened and he pulled her inside. She clawed at the masculine arm that held her.

"Do not scream, Miss Westfall. You are in no danger."

Daphne twisted free of his hold and lunged for the door. He yanked her onto the seat opposite him.

"Miss Westfall, please. I am attempting to render aid."

She stilled at his urgency. He was the too-handsome man she had glimpsed across the street. How had he gotten behind her so quickly?

"Render aid?" she demanded, hating how frightened she sounded. "Kidnapping is not the kind of aid I require."

"That's fortunate, for it's not the aid I'm offering." He

released her arm and leaned back against the cushion. "My name is Sir Anthony Heathcoat. Some call me The Lord of Arrangements."

"The Lord of Arrangements?" She had never heard of him. "What does this have to do with me?"

He smiled gently. "Everything."

She studied him. His expression lacked pity or lust. Perhaps his aid was nothing more than letting her rest inside a warm coach, away from the icy winds.

"I know about your father," Anthony said.

Daphne tensed. He wasn't the first man to seek vengeance on her because of her father.

"Easy, lass," He lifted a hand. "I've no desire to harm you. Allow me to speak. Afterwards, if you don't wish for my help, I will allow you to return to your position on the street with an extra few pounds for your trouble."

Shame heated her face and she glanced away. Never in her life had she believed she would be sitting in a coach with a man discussing her life as a beggar.

She raised her chin and met his gaze. No threatening shadow darkened his eyes. "Very well. Speak your piece."

"I am aware of your father's crimes," he said. "Counterfeiting is a serious offense. He's lucky they didn't send him to the gallows."

Daphne tried to swallow the sudden lump in her throat.

"I also know that his conviction resulted in his property being used to repay his victims; at least, those who were members of the peerage."

Another painful gulp. She couldn't speak. That had been the worst indignity. Her father had betrayed friends in society, tainting them with his dishonor. She had not been allowed to hear the more gruesome details from her father's solicitor, but she had heard whispers that one man had shot himself after being associated with the scandal.

"I have never believed the sins of the father should pass to his children," he said. "It is unjust that you should suffer for his crimes. I wish to help you."

"How can you?" she asked, feeling strangely numb.

"Have you noticed how the *ton* always favors a good marriage? The right union can erase even the worst sins from public memory." He smiled. "Perhaps even for someone shadowed by scandal."

Shadowed by Scandal? The man had a way with words. But marriage? No sane man would marry her. Even the shabbiest modistes had refused to employ her as a simple seamstress because her family name was so blackened.

"But... I have no prospects, no connections. No gentleman would ever—"

Anthony's soft chuckle stunned her into silence. "No need to fret, Miss Westfall. I am quite convinced I can find half a dozen men who would consider it a privilege to take you as a wife. If you are agreeable, that is."

"Agreeable?" she repeated. Perhaps it was warmer in the coach then she'd realized, for her head began to swim.

"A marriage auction," he said. "Polite society doesn't discuss this form of...courtship, but the general arrangement is this: you meet the interested gentlemen, then they bid for your hand."

"Bid?" The word escaped in a frightened squeak.

Anthony nodded. "The money they bid will be placed in a secure trust for your use. Contracts are signed and a male trustee of your choosing is appointed to ensure your husband honors the terms. This provides you with money to live comfortably. Of course, one hopes, your new husband will offer you even more as his wife."

It sounded mad, but... Daphne bit her lip as she considered. An arranged marriage? Women of title and wealth were contracted in marriage to men who offered the best terms.

But she wasn't a woman of wealth. And to be sold into marriage? She stared at the roof of the carriage. Put that way, it sounded little better than the White House Brothel. Still, allowing a stranger to bid on her? Marry her? Could she agree to something so wild?

"Would...would there be a way to ensure these candidates are not prone to hurting their wives? I could not marry someone who..." She trailed off. She'd learned men could be cruel and abusive if it suited their desires, and she had no wish to give away her relative safety in marriage to a man who would hurt her. She'd seen evidence of that enough when she'd witnessed a woman accosted the other night on the street and robbed of her coins. The man who'd stolen from her had beaten her severely and no one had stepped in to help her because she was a prostitute.

His expression sobered. "Of course. I will conduct a most detailed interview of the candidates, and you will have my word, only good men will bid upon you."

She slid her hand into her dress pocket and stroked the smooth pearls. "You really think men will bid upon a...woman shadowed by scandal?"

Anthony nodded. "The men will be aware of your situation, and I can assure that they will not judge you for it."

Anthony smiled and Daphne was startled at the kindness in his expression. "Not all men judge a woman for her father's crimes." A twinkle appeared in his eyes. "Especially when she is intelligent—and beautiful."

Heat crept up her cheeks. "When must I decide?" she asked.

"I can give you a week, but I would prefer that you weren't wandering the streets. You could catch your death. If you agreed now, I can have the auction proceed as early as tomorrow and provide you a warm bed for the night, along with hot food."

Her stomach cramped at the mere thought of food. She should fear this stranger's motives—she should decline and flee, but instinct--or intuition--urged her to trust this man. She pressed a hand to her stomach. Or maybe it was starvation that overrode common sense. "Please, consider accepting now," he said.

She studied his earnest face in the dim confines of the coach. "What do you gain by helping me?"

Anthony didn't reply immediately, but she noted a hint of melancholy that dimmed the earlier glint in his eyes. "I find that bringing people together, people who suit, gives me purpose. Too many people focus on money and power. I want to create a force for love." He grinned and suddenly looked years younger. "A tad romantic, I know, but I cannot help myself. I have a certain talent for bringing couples together, and often they end up in love matches."

Love... Daphne hadn't thought of love in so long, she questioned whether such an emotion still existed. Anthony might have a talent for making matches, but she would never be fortunate enough to find love. But a man who cared for her even a little—a man who wanted children... Oh my, she hadn't considered that possibility. Such a man would provide a life far beyond anything she'd dared hope. For the last several months, she'd felt frozen in a way that had nothing to do with wind and snow . . .unable to move, to change her fate in any way.

"I...I will do it," she said at last, her tone strong despite her racing heart.

"Wonderful! Do you have any possessions we need to fetch, or can we go straight to the house?"

"I have nothing save what I am wearing," she admitted, another blush of shame warming her face.

"Not to worry," Anthony said, but the sorrow in his eyes was almost too much to bear. She focused on the small window of the coach while he opened the door and gave the driver an address.

A marriage auction. But what choice had she? She pressed her hand against the pearls hidden in her dress and closed her eyes. The edges of her frozen world seemed to thaw just a bit, and her body warmed with the promise of safety and a chance to live again.

2

Lachlan Grant strode into the card room of Berkley's club, scowling at any man who dared appear to think about getting in his way. The coach ride from Edinburgh had been long and tedious and he wasn't in the mood to deal with foppish Englishmen preening before one another. He didn't even wish to be out this evening, but remaining alone one moment longer in his brother's townhouse would have driven him insane.

No, no longer his brother's...

Like everything else in the months since his older brother's death, that residence still felt like William's. William's title, William's home, William's life. Lachlan had simply stepped into his boots to fill the void.

I never wanted to be the Earl of Huntley.

A bitter taste clung to his tongue and he scowled, his mood blackening further.

Now he was saddled with a bloody title and all the duties and responsibilities that came attached. He had gained a fortune he'd never wanted, and the price had been the brother he'd treasured most.

Lachlan scanned the tables, desperate to join any card game, even though his heart rebelled. He felt reckless, angry, and ready to do something utterly foolish--*anything* to ease the ache in his chest.

He was the last of the Grant family, for neither he nor William had married. It was one of the reasons they had been so close, only two years apart in age. William had turned thirty a mere six months before he'd passed, and Lachlan had just turned eight and twenty, far too young to lose his brother.

A burst of laughter from a nearby table drew his focus. A group of young bucks leaned around a Faro table, excited by their winnings. He started toward the table, but someone stepped into his path and he stumbled into the man.

"My apologies," he muttered.

The other man caught him by the shoulders and they both stood back. Lachlan blinked in surprise as he recognized that dark hair and angled chin. "Anthony?" The dark clouds gathering on his inner horizon lifted somewhat.

"My God, Lachlan!" Sir Anthony Heathcoat slapped him on the shoulder in greeting. "How long has it been?"

"At least four months," Lachlan chuckled.

His friend sighed but his eyes remained warm. "Four months? That long? You've been well, I trust?" This question came more carefully and Lachlan knew why. Anthony had been just as close to William as he was to Lachlan, but he'd been out of the country and had missed the funeral. William's unexpected death had left many of their friends still coping with his loss.

"I admit, I have been better." Lachlan scrubbed a hand along his jaw. "Never wanted to run Huntley Castle. Not that I have a choice now."

Anthony nodded, his eyes shadowed. "Come and have a drink. I want your opinion on something."

Lachlan followed Anthony. Encountering his old friend had softened his reckless mood. They entered a quiet reading room with a crackling fire and thick plush chairs. After settling, Anthony waved a boy over and ordered two glasses of brandy.

Lachlan rested his forearms on his knees and leaned close to Anthony. "What can you possibly need my advice on?"

Anthony met his gaze with a sudden hint of mischief. "I'm holding a marriage auction tomorrow evening. I was hoping you might join us and bid on the bride."

A bark of laughter escaped Lachlan, but he sobered when his friend frowned. "What the devil is a marriage auction?"

His friend chuckled. "It's exactly as it sounds. I have a lovely young lady staying at my home and I'm inviting some marriage-minded men to meet her and speak with her for a few minutes. Then you bid upon her. The highest bidder takes her as a bride. The money he bids is placed in a special trust for the lady, to be handled by a third party, a man she trusts and chooses."

"The women involved are willing participants?"

Anthony drew back. "What do you take me for?"

"A far better man than I just implied. I apologize. So, tell me, what is this actually about?"

"It's about aiding ladies in distress, women who are desperate for a match. Most men agree to pay a small fortune to secure a bride."

"And you have men agreeing to purchase a bride?" Lachlan never thought to meet a man willing to give a fortune to a wife when the law allowed husbands to claim their wives' property. Lachlan wasn't one to marry for monetary gain, but he knew many men did.

"You'd be surprised. Not every man is as jaded as you about love, old friend. Some are quite happy to find a sweet young woman to marry so that they might make a good life together. Now..." Anthony paused as the boy returned with their brandy on a tray. Once he departed, Anthony said, "Now, would you consider coming and bidding on the woman?"

"Bid on a bride? You want me to *buy* a woman? God's teeth, Anthony, I have no wish to marry yet. Besides, I have no need to buy a wife, you know that." Mere weeks after William's death, women were seeking invitations to visit him in Scotland. Half of the English *ton* wanted to traipse across his threshold, invade his life and disturb his grief, all for the chance of leg-shackling the newest Earl of Huntley.

Anthony sipped his brandy, eyeing Lachlan thoughtfully. "I remember all too well your wilder days, but with William gone, a wife might ease some of your burden."

Lachlan frowned and swirled the contents of his glass.

His friend's eyes narrowed. "You know I didn't mean it that way."

They drank in silence for a moment before Anthony shrugged off the tension and smiled. "I thought you might be interested in knowing that the young lady is Daphne Westfall. She's very beautiful and quite sweet. I was hoping you would at least consider meeting her."

Westfall...

The name hit him like a blow to the gut...a name carved in blood upon his heart. On the study table near his brother's body had been a letter that explained the shame and responsibility William felt over his dealings with the notorious counterfeiter Sir Richard Westfall. The Huntley title and lands had survived the fallout from Westfall's forgeries, but William had never been one to withstand the loss of honor.

"Westfall?" Lachlan's mouth ran dry at the name. "She wouldn't happen to be Sir Richard's daughter, would she? The man convicted of counterfeiting bank notes?"

Anthony gave a slow nod. "Indeed, she is. Do you know her?"

Lachlan had never shared the contents of the letter with anyone, not even his mother.

"No, but I hear she is a nice lass, despite her father's crimes."

He'd heard no such thing. Hadn't even known the old bastard had a child. But the revenge he never thought he'd get for William might now wait within reach.

"So, you'll come? I promised Miss Westfall I would bring good, decent men to bid on her. She's fallen on hard times, and a good match would secure her future."

Lachlan composed his features into a polite show of interest. "Of course. I'd be happy to meet the lass and bid on her."

Heathcoat grinned. "Marriage will suit you well. I had a feeling it would take only a nudge."

With a grim smile, Lachlan agreed. Sir Richard was in prison for his crimes, and so would his daughter endure a prison of another sort.

She was going to marry him, and spend the rest of her life paying for her father's crimes by forgoing the rich trappings that her father's forgeries had given her. She would learn to live with no frivolity, no joy, no love...nothing.

Just as he was condemned to live without his brother.

We can suffer together.

Daphne felt like an imposter in the blue gown that Anthony had given her. He'd insisted she keep it, but she'd promised she would find a way to return it once she had new clothes of her own. Fear turned her mouth bitter as she tried not to think about her future after tonight, and she reached instinctively for the pearls in the pocket of her new gown.

As she entered the drawing room of Anthony Heathcoat's townhouse, she reminded herself that this was the safest option remaining. If she secured a husband tonight, she would avoid the brothel and not go hungry again.

A group of seven men stood by the fire, all talking quietly to one another. When she cleared her throat, they turned as one, each instantly assessing her. She folded her hands in front of her to control their shaking as she endured their speculative perusals.

She'd never thought much of how brood mares felt when being sold at Tattersals, but now she felt quite sorry for the creatures.

"Gentlemen, may I present Miss Daphne Westfall?" Anthony approached, lifted one of her hands to his lips and kissed her gloved fingers. "Are you all right, my dear?" he whispered.

"Yes, I just feel a little..." Her trembling hand said what she could not. He gave it a gentle squeeze.

"They are good men and will treat you fairly."

"Thank you," she said. She meant it. Anthony had saved her from the streets and she would never be able to repay his kindness.

"Good. I will introduce you to each man. They will place their bids in their envelopes. The highest bidder will return and we will sign the contracts. This will secure your monetary assets."

Daphne's throat constricted. She still couldn't believe she was really doing this, meeting with men in hopes that they would want to marry her. How was this different from prostituting herself? At least, she shared her body with only one man, and she didn't live with the shame of a brothel address.

"Gentlemen, please form a line so I may make your introductions to Miss Westfall."

The men formed a queue, and one by one she was

presented to each. They were all charming, friendly, and genuine. With each introduction, she grew more relieved. She had a minute or two to speak with them and found she liked each one. Anthony had kept his promise.

The last man who approached her was different. She had to tilt her head back to see his face. He was incredibly tall, with broad shoulders. She felt tiny in his presence. He was a little more muscular than the others and a bit intimidating. She almost retreated a step, if only to see his face better.

"Miss Westfall, this is Lachlan Grant, the Earl of Huntley."

"It is a pleasure," Lachlan's deep voice was heavy with a Scottish brogue.

"My Lord," she replied, staring into his dark blue eyes. They were a lovely deep sapphire, yet a strange gleam flashed in their depths and then vanished behind a polite smile. Had she merely imagined that? Perhaps so. She had heard more than once that Scotsmen tended to be brooding and intense, and it seemed Huntley was no different.

"You're from Scotland? Whereabouts, if I may ask?"

"The town of Huntley is a half day's ride north of Edinburgh." His eyes remained locked on her with an almost predatory gaze. She shivered, trying to think of how to continue their conversation and draw out more of his personality.

"I've never been north of Edinburgh. I imagine it must be lovely."

There it was, a momentary softening of his eyes and mouth. "Aye, 'tis stunning, especially in the spring when the heather blooms."

"Would we live there most of the year, if your bid is successful?" It was something she asked of each gentleman. She needed a home, a place she could feel safe, a place to escape the judgment of the *ton* for her father's crimes.

"We would. I only visit London once or twice a year. Would that suit you?" he asked.

"Yes, whatever you do will be fine for me, I'm quite sure." A home in the Highlands...she loved the idea, but she wasn't sure she was ready to marry someone as serious and brooding as the man who stood before her.

"Now," Anthony smiled at the men. "Place your bids, and then please wait outside." Several of the men offered Daphne warm, hopeful smiles before writing down their bids and sealing their envelopes.

Daphne's gaze was drawn to Lachlan as he scratched his numbers on the bit of paper he held. His eyes met hers and a bolt of shock ran through her as if she were *owned* by him in that instant. The sensation frightened her and yet she couldn't look away from him even as he placed his envelope on Anthony's palm and strode from the room.

The final men handed their envelopes to Anthony before leaving the room. After the last man left, Anthony and his manservant, Finchley, opened the bids. Daphne watched them rearrange the pieces of paper in order as the higher bids moved to the top. Her heart pounded so hard against her ribs that she had trouble breathing. Which of the strangers was to be her husband?

"Ahh, here we are." Anthony glanced her way. "We have our winner. I shall thank the others and send them home." Anthony exited the room. The click of the door sounded far too loud in the awkward silence. Daphne clutched the edge of a chair for support, her nails digging into the floral pattern of the fabric as she struggled to calm herself.

The door opened and Daphne sucked in a breath. Sir Anthony entered, followed by the Earl of Huntley. Once again, she became the focus of that brooding gaze. Wasn't he pleased to have been the highest bidder? The tight purse of his lips suggested otherwise. A pit formed in her stomach and she struggled to breathe. She was to marry him...the man who spoke of Highland heather in the spring, but who looked like a wolf about to devour her. Which was his true nature? Perhaps he was a man torn between his duality of nature. Perhaps she might never know the real Lachlan Grant.

Anthony approached her while Huntley waited inside the door, hands folded behind his back like a military general.

Oh dear...

"Miss Westfall, Lord Huntley was by far the highest bidder at fifteen thousand pounds, which he has agreed to place into an account where the trustee of your choice will oversee the funds for you."

Daphne barely listened. Instead, she stared at Huntley and he at her. A slow smile curved his lips. It was not a cruel smile, no, but it warned her that she was pledging herself to a wolf. She was tempted to look away, to yield to that dominating stare, but she held her ground and lifted her chin.

Yet her instincts warned her to run far and fast from Lord Huntley.

"Sir... Anthony, may I have a minute to speak with you?" she asked, her voice wavering. Huntley shared a look with Anthony before he nodded and left the room.

Anthony approached, concern in his eyes. "You're trembling. Are you all right?"

"Lord Huntley, is he a good man? You promise that I'm safe with him?"

"I promise," Anthony vowed. "Huntley is a long-time friend. I would trust him with my life. He's rich and has excellent lands—"

"I don't care about that. I care about *him*. Is he the sort of man to care for his wife? Not...harm her?" She bravely forced the question out, even knowing it was not polite to speak of such matters.

"He's never harmed a woman. If he seems a bit cold, it's

because his older brother, William, died only two months ago. He was close to William. His brother's death changed him, hardened him in some ways. But I promise you, he is a good man."

She saw only honesty in Anthony's eyes and she trusted that more than anything else. "Very well then, I agree to marry him."

"Good." Anthony then called for Huntley, who reentered the room. They assembled about the card table, where Finchley laid out several documents.

"Here's the trust agreement, Huntley. I filled out the forms with the amount you bid. All you need do is sign, as will Miss Westfall. Finchley and I will witness the contracts to assure they are binding."

Daphne watched Huntley bend over the table and scrawl his name before he straightened and held the quill out to her. She accepted it, her gloved fingers brushing his. A spark of heat flared between them, and just as quickly vanished. Huntley's eyes darted away as he stepped back. She leaned over the table and penned her own name.

"Excellent. Huntley, you can collect Miss Westfall tomorrow after you have procured a special license."

"Actually, I would like to marry in Scotland, unless the lady objects." Huntley looked to Daphne.

"Marry in Scotland?" Daphne had to force strength into her voice. She hadn't expected to leave so soon.

There's nothing to tie you here, not anymore.

"Aye, there's a little church not far from Huntley Castle. It's tradition for the men of the Grant family to marry there."

"Oh... I suppose that would be all right." She had no friends left in London, none that would be seen with her. She had no real reason to stay here. In fact, it was quite possible that if word got out about her wedding, the victims of her father would come to the church and make trouble on her wedding day.

"We are agreed then?" Huntley asked. His blue eyes seemed to swallow her whole.

"Yes." With that single word, she felt she sealed a bargain with the devil. A most handsome, intimidating devil...

"The paperwork is all in order," Anthony said. "Anyone care for a glass of sherry to celebrate?"

Huntley shook his head. "Not tonight, old friend. I have a wedding to prepare for."

Anthony turned to Daphne. "What about you? Sherry, my dear?"

"Yes, please," she whispered. She needed a drink.

Huntley approached, grasped her hand and raised it to his lips. Their eyes met and held once again.

"Tomorrow," he promised softly.

"Tomorrow," she echoed. Then with a kiss to her knuckles that left her body burning with a strange sensation, he left the room.

Daphne watched him go, wondering if what she had agreed to would save her or damn her.

3

Lachlan climbed out of his coach the following morning, stretched his legs, and climbed the steps of Anthony's townhouse. He paused at the door, holding his breath for a moment. The moment he went inside, his life would change forever. He knew that he could turn and run from this, change his mind about his plans, yet he didn't. Every emotion that had raged the night before was now locked away in a dark corner of his mind. Instead of focusing on his brother's death and the man responsible, he focused instead on the woman, Daphne, the bastard's daughter.

When he stood there in the drawing room the night before, as nervous as the other men, he had hated himself for showing such weakness. And then she had entered, a tiny creature with soft curves, dark hair and warm brown eyes. She had been as timid as a dormouse, her eyes as round as saucers as she'd gone through the introductions. Missing was the spoiled hellion he had expected from a man like Sir Richard Westfall.

He *wanted* to despise her on sight and rally his vengeance, but it hadn't been easy to hate her. He had managed it, but only just.

Lachlan growled in frustration as he rapped the knocker of the door. A moment later, a butler answered.

"I'm here for Miss Westfall," he announced. The butler nodded and opened the door wider, allowing him to step into the vestibule.

"Ahh. There you are, Huntley!" Anthony descended the stairs, Miss Westfall at his side. She wore a soft green carriage gown with a blue satin sash around her waist. The colors emphasized her dark hair and alabaster skin. Lachlan clenched his teeth as his body responded to her subtle beauty. He did not want to desire this woman, but perhaps he could allow himself that one weakness. She would be his wife, after all, and he did plan to beget heirs upon her. It was his duty now, and hers as his wife.

"Anthony," Lachlan greeted his friend with more warmth than he felt for Miss Westfall.

Her eyes were downcast, her lips parted, and for a brief instant he caught a glimpse of a woman beaten down, her spirit already broken. That was what he had wished for, wasn't it? A broken woman? Yet he'd wanted to break her himself, not collect the pieces with pity.

"Are you ready to leave?" he asked her. "I suppose you have quite a few clothes and other possessions to take with you."

At this, she raised her eyes and he saw sorrow in their honey brown depths.

"I have none. Even this gown is borrowed." She plucked at the skirts, revealing two dainty black boots.

"Borrowed?" he echoed with shock. How was it she had no clothes, no possessions? Surely that damned criminal of a father had left her plenty to live on.

"Yes. I... I thought you understood the circumstances I

was in, my lord. I would not have agreed to the auction otherwise."

Lachlan was left speechless, until his friend gave a short cough.

"Er... Huntley, might I have a word with you?" Anthony jerked his head toward the door and released Miss Westfall's arm so he and Lachlan could talk in private.

"What is the meaning of this? Where are her clothes?" Lachlan growled. He had no desire to buy anything for the woman. His entire plan of revenge called for doing the exact opposite, allowing her barely enough to survive.

"Huntley, I didn't want to mention this, since it seems to be a delicate matter, but the reason I held the auction was to get the poor woman off the streets."

"The streets?" Miss Westfall had been selling her body to survive? "You promised me a bride, not a trollop."

Anthony's eyes flashed dangerously. "She isn't one. She was, I suspect, considering the possibility when I came across her. She was standing in an alley, scrambling for coins tossed her way. Do you have any idea what she must have gone through? A gentle born lady left begging for scraps?"

The pain in Anthony's eyes was genuine, and Lachlan wondered how bad off Miss Westfall really was. He glanced over his shoulder at his future bride, who stood at the foot of the stairs, eyes once more downcast, one hand tucked in the pocket of her gown.

"You must take care of her. I know that William's death has been hard on you, but perhaps this marriage will heal you--heal you both."

Heal him? Nothing could mend the bleeding bits of his tattered heart. William's loss had left a gaping hole inside him, and nothing and no one could ever fill that.

Lachlan turned and walked past Miss Westfall toward the

door. "We should be going. We have a long journey ahead of us."

She looked up at his approach, and for a second he saw hope in her eyes, calling to him, but he smashed down the urge to respond in kind.

"Ready?" he asked coldly.

She nodded and looked at his arm expectantly. He did not offer it.

Anthony called to him as they stepped outside, "Huntley, I meant what I said."

Lachlan did not reply as he opened the coach door for his acquisition. She climbed inside and he followed, settling back on the seat opposite her.

The coach rattled into motion and for a long while Lachlan wouldn't look at her. He kept picturing her in a tattered gown, ankle-deep in icy water as carriages and people passed, no one looking her way, no one caring about her. He mentally gave himself a shake.

I will not pity her, I will not let this creature crawl beneath my skin.

She was the daughter of a man who had destroyed many lives, a man in prison for crimes that had led William to take his own life.

Lachlan felt her gaze on him and, at last, looked her way.

"What?" he demanded in irritation.

"Why did you do it?" she asked, her head tilting as if in puzzlement.

He crossed his arms over his chest. "Do what?"

"Bid on me. It's abundantly clear that you do not like me. Why did you attend the auction? Have you had second thoughts? You had plenty of time after seeing me to walk away. You did not have to write anything down on that paper. I would've been happy to go with any of the other gentlemen."

The thought of her going home with another man, of having his vengeance denied, filled him with quiet rage.

"I wanted you. That's why I placed my bid." His growling response would have made any sensible woman know that the discussion was over. But not Daphne. The timidity he'd seen in her the previous night wasn't there anymore.

"You certainly aren't acting like a man who wants me." She seemed to regret what she said. "I don't mean—"

"Oh, I *want* you, lass. I have no doubt that I'll enjoy bedding you." He managed a sardonic smile that caused her to lean away from him. He chuckled darkly at her reaction.

"Don't be afraid. I won't touch you until we are properly wed, and only when I'm certain you want me too."

Her face flushed red and she sucked in a breath. "You mustn't talk so openly of—"

"Of bedding? Lass, you'd best get used to it. We Scots aren't so squeamish as you English."

"I really must insist you do not do that with me."

"Do what?" he challenged with a wicked grin. The more he teased her, the more that other version of himself seemed to return, the rogue who would take her in his arms and kiss her senseless right here in this coach.

"Please don't tease me about..."

"Sex? Miss Westfall, I'm a man with appetites, and I plan to teach you to have your own as well." He couldn't help it. He moved to the seat beside her and reached up to cup her face. She tensed and tried to withdraw. He may have planned for misery in her married life, but he wasn't as cold hearted as to make her unhappy in his bed. Even he had limits.

"Stop resisting, lass," he said, and he loved the way her eyes flashed in open defiance.

"I'm not resisting, nor am I willing." She growled softly, the sound reminiscent of an angry cat he'd once startled in a barn as a boy. He'd learned then that cats had dangerous claws.

"I said I wouldna do anything to you and I meant it. But damned if you don't need a kiss to cool that temper of yours."

She arched a brow and knocked his hand away from her face. Then she moved to the other side of the coach, scowling at him. "I would not have a temper if you would behave like a proper gentleman."

He let her go, keeping to the promise that he wouldn't touch her until she was willing. He was a bastard for marrying her for revenge, but he was not a devil and would never force a woman to do anything she didn't wish to when it came to sex. Still, he saw the flush of color in her cheeks and the way her breath had quickened. She'd been aroused, even if she was angry at him for teasing her. Now he was looking forward to what it would be like to give her pleasure. His body was already humming with the prospect.

I could teach her to want me when I so choose, and leave her without my touch when it suits me.

He would derive some satisfaction knowing he could leave her aching for him whenever he wanted to. She blushed again and glanced out the coach window, clearly determined to avoid him and the subject of sex. There was a fair amount of amusement to provoking her humility and embarrassment and he would take his humor when he could.

She continued to ignore him and he let her. She would panic when she realized that they would not be sleeping in separate rooms tonight. The little chit would squirm because she hadn't yet realized that she had no maid and he would have to be the one to undress her.

Time passed as the coach continued north. Daphne fidgeted in her seat and tried to sleep against the side of the coach. He had left his more comfortable conveyance back at

Huntley Castle. Not that he should be concerned with her comfort, that wasn't part of his revenge.

She finally settled with a soft sigh, her eyes closing. At first, he'd wanted to crow in triumph, but the expression on her face gave him pause. Her full lips tilted down in an open frown and a little wrinkle of worry creased her sleeping brow. A ripple of guilt disturbed him enough that he continued to stare at her for some time.

When he was convinced she was fast asleep, he reached over and lifted her onto his lap. She tensed. For an instant, he feared he'd woken her, but then she relaxed and burrowed deeper into his arms. His body was taut with arousal, but he suppressed his baser urges and instead focused on her weight and warmth in his arms. She was the daughter of the man who had driven William to suicide, yet here she was, lying in his arms, trusting him not to hurt her, trusting that he would be a good husband.

Will I?

The question had an easy answer.

I would've been...before.

But losing William had broken him and his mother. Their original family of four was now two, and here he was bringing home the child of the man who had brought death to their home. He'd kept the truth of William's involvement in Westfall's counterfeiting a secret. As far as his mother knew, William had killed himself but left no reason as to why. Lachlan didn't want his mother filled with the same vengeance that burned inside of him. If his mother ever discovered Daphne's true identity, she would cast her out. Therefore, Lachlan could not tell her who Daphne was. The burden of losing a child in such a way was torture enough, and he did not want to add to that misery.

Plagued by worries, he leaned his head back and tried to sleep, still cradling Daphne in his arms. When sleep came, dreams consumed him, dreams that made his heart bleed and his throat hoarse with silent screams. Yet buried beneath the nightmares of losing his brother lay a warm softness against him that brought comfort.

"Sleep in the stables?" Daphne whispered to Lachlan, facing away from the frowning innkeeper. They were a day's ride from Scotland, and there wasn't another inn for miles. They couldn't press on because of the storm that had blown in and still raged.

"'Tis the only space left," the innkeeper insisted. "The rain, you see. Everyone stopped here. The roads are bad for miles around."

Lachlan glanced away and she swallowed hard.

"Can you tolerate some hay, lass?" he asked, his tone cool.

She nodded stiffly. They'd woken up in each other's arms only half an hour before, in a strange and wonderful sort of intimacy that had shocked her. His hold had been protective and gentle, his eyes soft and inviting. Yet here he was, treating her coldly again. What was she supposed to do?

Lachlan slapped down several fat coins on the counter "Then we'll take the loft, but I'm not paying full price." The innkeeper collected them and slipped them into his apron pocket.

He led them to a muddy courtyard, where icy rain pelted their skin before they reached the protection of the stables. Over a dozen horses were tucked away in stalls. The warm scents of hay and grain were oddly comforting to Daphne as she kept pace with Lachlan.

"Use this ladder," the innkeeper said, "and be careful not to roll off the ledge in the night." The innkeeper retrieved several thick woolen blankets and offered them to Lachlan, who took them under one arm.

Lachlan turned to Daphne. "You go first. I'll be here to catch you if you slip." He gave her a gentle nudge. She approached the wooden ladder, a tad apprehensive. Heights were not something she enjoyed.

"Go on, lass," Lachlan growled and gave her bottom a gentle swat.

"How dare you!" She was torn between mortification and anger, both emotions almost choking her. The innkeeper laughed at her sputter of outrage.

"Climb, or I'll do it again," Lachlan warned with a twinkle in his eyes that she didn't like. The swat hadn't hurt, of course, not with the layers she wore, but to strike a lady in such an intimate place, especially when they weren't alone...

Daphne clenched her teeth, used one hand to lift her skirts and the other to climb. She had to go slow. When she reached the top, she toppled over into a mountain of fresh hay. There was space for both her and Lachlan to sleep, but not much more than that. She stilled as she realized that she and Lachlan would be sleeping mere inches apart.

Nerves stormed the inside of her belly and she fought off a little shiver. *We're not married yet.*

Lachlan emerged over the edge of the loft and tossed the blankets to her. She caught them and waited until he knelt beside her amid the mountains of hay.

"Make yourself a nest and get some rest. I'll find some dinner." He tucked the blankets more fully into her lap before he shifted back toward the loft's edge. She set the bedding aside and stepped toward him.

"Lachlan—"

He paused, already halfway off the ledge. "Aye?"

Suddenly tongue-tied, Daphne blushed. She wasn't sure

what she'd meant to say, only that she'd wanted to say something.

"Be careful not to fall."

He answered her warning with an inscrutable expression before dropping from view.

Once he left, she arranged the hay to lay more evenly, then spread one blanket as a bottom sheet and the second as a cover. It would have to do.

She almost laughed. Of course, it would do. It would do very well. This bed was a far better accommodation than she'd had these last two months. There was nothing so dreadful as curling up in the nook of a doorway or huddling beneath bushes in Hyde Park. Those were the places she'd grown accustomed to sleeping. Here she had a roof over her head and warm blankets. By comparison, it would be easy to endure, even if they went hungry tonight. Given the crowds due to the storm, it was possible the inn might run out of food, as well.

She settled back in the hay, curled into a ball and closed her eyes. She listened to the pattering rain on the stable roof and the rustle and occasion snort of the horses below. There was a gentle cadence to it all that exuded a sense of peace. Since her father's incarceration, she'd carried the weight of his sins squarely upon her shoulders. Yet now, at this moment, that burden was lessened. Daphne inhaled slowly and let her thoughts turn to the future, to Lachlan.

He was a Scottish earl, with a vast estate in Scotland, yet he'd agreed to marry an English woman who Sir Heathcoat had made clear was in need of financial support. What sort of man agreed to that? Was he desperate for a wife?

The ladder to the loft creaked and Daphne squeaked in surprise, clutching the blanket to her chest, even though she remained fully dressed.

"I dinnae mean to scare you," Lachlan chuckled as he

appeared at the loft edge. He reached up and set down a tray containing covered dishes.

She stared at the fully laden tray in awe. "How did you carry that?"

"It wasn't hard, a wee bit of balance was all." He joined her in the makeshift bed and they shared the food in a quaint silence. Lachlan was clearly not a talkative man, which Daphne did regret. She had loved to talk to her father and her friends...before everything had gone wrong.

"Have more travelers arrived?" she asked.

"Aye. There will be no beds, and likely the stables will fill up, as well. We'll have to stay in the loft unless that distresses your delicate feminine sensibilities." The sudden coldness in his tone surprised her.

"Oh, no, here's quite fine," she rushed to assure him. Perhaps his pride had been pricked by having to sleep above animals in a stable.

"I know you are used to finer things, but let me warn you, sweet bride," his tone was still cold and she shivered. "There will be no fine clothes or expensive things in Huntley. It is not my way and it won't be yours."

Daphne didn't miss the way he said this. Each word seemed to have a dreadful importance to it, but she couldn't see why. She was not foolish enough to ask for an explanation.

"I'm quite accustomed to going without," she murmured.

"Having to borrow a dress or two isn't going without." His tone was now angry and a fierce scowl crossed his face. It might have made her flinch, but she was safe and warm and fed for the first time in days, aside from her night spent in Anthony's home. She wasn't going to let Lachlan bully her, even with words.

"I have gone without," she said, her tone as hard as steel. "Did your friend not tell you? He found me begging in the streets, my only gown ripped, my belly empty, and my limbs frozen."

She paused. Her body practically shook with fury. How dare he assume she was some spoiled child who'd never faced hardship? "For the last two months, I would've given *anything* to have a roof and a dry place to lay my head. I was on the verge of..." She choked on the words, but his silent stare dared her to continue. "I was going that very night to a brothel, my last hope for food and a warm bed." She drank the last of her wine in a long gulp and stared at him hard. "But Anthony found me. He rescued me before I made that mistake. Do not *ever* lecture me on going without, Lord Huntley. I have been ripped from my home. My life was destroyed because my father was careless and cavalier when it came to the law. I am paying for his sins. I only hope you, my future husband, will not judge me for them."

She kept her composure as she turned her back and lay down on the bed she'd made. That tiny distance was the only barrier she could make between them and she hoped he would respect it.

Only then did the tears she'd held back begin to flow. She heard him mutter something that sounded like a curse before he lay down beside her and curled one arm around her waist. He pulled her back a few inches to nestle her into the curve of his body. Of course, he wouldn't leave her alone. Even now, after all she had said, he wanted to remind her that he owned her. That she was bought and paid for. She tensed and tried to pull away from him, but she was tired and cold.

"I'm sorry, lass."

The words surprised her, but only half as much as the kiss he placed upon her cheek. The tenderness of it startled her enough that she shifted onto her back to stare at him.

"Why must you be so cruel, Lord Huntley?"

His blue eyes filled with shadows. "I... I am angry. Very

angry at someone and it keeps my temper short." His cryptic response was apologetic, but it was clear he would speak no more on the matter.

"You shouldn't hold on to anger, my lord. It doesn't help." She too had held onto anger for a long time. Anger at her father. But all too soon she realized anger didn't provide shelter, get her friends back, and didn't fill her belly.

"When a man's heart is broken, sometimes anger is all he has left." Lachlan's words were hoarse with emotion. Was he speaking of the brother he'd lost? Or was there more? Had he loved a woman and lost her?

"Go to sleep." His tone was even now. "We've a long journey ahead of us."

Daphne was certain there was no way she could sleep, not with the frantic pulse of her thoughts, but somewhere close to dawn, sleep did claim her.

NOTHING WAS GOING ACCORDING TO PLAN.

Lachlan scowled in the darkness of the loft as he held Daphne close for warmth. They had no proper room to share and neither of them had been able to bathe or change into nightclothes. They slept with animals. He'd wanted to be in control of her misery, to exact revenge on his terms, but the opportunities failed to appear.

Of course, after what she'd just told him, he couldn't shake the guilt of wanting his revenge. The need to avenge William was as strong as ever, but now there was a compulsion to protect Daphne, to care for her, which warred with his need for vengeance.

How can I protect her from me? He should send her back to London and let Anthony find one of those other love-struck lads who bid on her and give her to one of them. But the thought of giving her away now? He couldn't. She would be *his* wife.

The anger which had been a part of him since William's death usually burned like wildfire, snapping and snarling as it devoured his soul in its greedy flames. But at this moment, that rage had become a single candle flame.

He nuzzled the nape of Daphne's neck, inhaling her sweet scent and feeling the silken tresses of her hair slide against his cheek. She let out a soft sigh and scooted back against him. One of her hands touched his where he'd wrapped it around her waist, and she laced her fingers through his. She wasn't awake, or she would not have done that, yet he almost smiled at the thought that she trusted him, at least in sleep.

"Have I made a mistake, lass?" he whispered, knowing she wouldn't hear. "Because I want to keep you?" He wanted to keep her, yes, but for the wrong reasons.

Daphne slowly turned, still asleep, and wrapped herself around him, her face pressed to his chest, her leg slipping between his as she clung to him. A sharp pain burst close to his heart as he held her. How could he hurt this woman? She was not the spoiled brat he had hoped to torture by denying her material possessions. No, Daphne was a fighter, a survivor, like him.

Had she been anyone else's daughter, he would have fallen in love with her then and there, but he couldn't. She was the reminder of everything he'd lost. It would be an insult to William's memory if Lachlan abandoned his revenge and fell in love with Westfall's daughter.

So, I am damned either way...

4

The following day, Daphne held her breath as she stepped out of the coach and faced Huntley Castle. It was a beautiful medieval grey stone house abutted by extensive gardens on either side. Much of what might have been old-fashioned in architectural style to some seemed classic to her, and not run down.

She wasn't sure what she'd believed his home would look like. A dank, dreary place, perhaps? This home was certainly not any of those things. Rather, despite the winter, it appeared to be bustling with life and color. Candles were lit in windows and servants moved about the grounds tending the gardens, preparing them for the spring, still many months away.

"Not what you expected?" Lachlan asked.

She ducked her head, but couldn't control her blush.

"I'm not quite sure what I was expecting, but it is lovely." She admired the towers and the stained-glass windows along one wing. Statues lined the gravel pathway up to the front entryway. Rosebushes, now dormant in the winter, would be stunning come spring.

Lachlan instructed their driver to attend to his luggage. She had none.

"This way." He didn't offer his arm, but stayed close as they walked up to the house. The door opened and a fleet of servants came out to greet them. The faces Daphne glimpsed were cheerful and curious, despite the black bands of morning on the arms of their uniforms. Their positive response to her gave Daphne a flutter of hope.

They might like me as their new mistress. I might be happy here, after all.

"Ahh, here we are," Lachlan greeted the servants warmly before he turned to her. "This is Mrs. Stewart, the housekeeper." He nodded to a matronly woman and then to a man in a black suit. "And Mr. Frampton is the butler. This is Miss Daphne Westfall," he informed the staff. "We are to be married as soon as possible."

"Married?" An older woman emerged through the doorway, her face mired with confusion. "You only left for London five days ago!"

Daphne had a moment to study the woman at the top of the steps. Her dark blue dress was adorned with a white apron of fine lace, which signified she was a woman of high social standing. Daphne's heart jumped into her throat as she recognized Lachlan's features in this woman's face.

"Daphne, this is my mother, Moira, the Dowager Countess of Huntley. Mother, this is Daphne Westfall." Lachlan finally offered Daphne his arm as he escorted her up to meet his mother. Lachlan's mother speared her son with a penetrating gaze, not hostile, but certainly unamused. Daphne might have laughed as she realized his mother was the one he'd inherited that intense stare from, but, at the moment, she was struggling to remember to breathe. Daphne resisted the urge to cling to Lachlan like a frightened child. It wasn't that she was afraid, but the shame of who she was and her family situation made her shift restlessly.

"Lachlan, you went to London to attend to business. You made no mention of an intent to find a bride." Lachlan's mother turned toward Daphne and suddenly smiled with genuine warmth. "It's wonderful to meet you, Daphne. I'm sorry we weren't ready to greet you, my dear. My son, as usual, forgot his manners and didn't send us any advanced notice."

"Oh please, don't be upset with him. We left London quickly and there wasn't time to write. It's nice to meet you." She dipped into a curtsey.

"Ach, an English lass," Moira chuckled and gave her son a rueful smile. "I suppose you never will do things as expected. Well, come inside, Miss Westfall. I'm sure you're tired after the long journey."

"Indeed, we are."

Lachlan and Daphne followed Moira into the house, which was even more beautiful than the outside. Cherrywood banisters with delicately carved spindles led to the upstairs corridors. High windows allowed sunlight to illuminate the portraits hanging on green satin walls. There was an unexpected brightness to the castle that surprised Daphne. With Lachlan's anger and grim moods, she'd expected to arrive at a dark estate sinking into the moors, not this place of sunlight and fresh air. It was clear that the house matched Moira rather than her son. She was a warm, smiling woman who had laugh lines around her eyes and mouth.

"Where shall we put Miss Westfall?" Mr. Frampton inquired of Lachlan.

"The blue room in the east wing," Moira said before her son could speak. Daphne didn't miss Lachlan's sudden frown. Was the blue room a good room or a bad one?

"If you follow me, miss," Mrs. Stewart said to Daphne, "I'll show you to your room."

"Rest and have a bath, Miss Westfall," Moira said. "We shall dine in an hour, if that suits you."

"Yes, that would be fine, thank you." Daphne peeked at Lachlan, but he was already striding away. The sight of his retreating form sent a flutter of panic through her. He was the only person in this castle she knew and he was already abandoning her.

"Don't fret, my dear," Moira gave her shoulder a motherly squeeze. "He'll be back soon enough. He never likes to let the dust of travel linger and is likely going to have a bath himself." Moira was still smiling but there was a hint of concern that transformed the laugh lines around her eyes into something akin to sorrow. Daphne knew why. She, too, sensed something wrong, but couldn't put her finger on what it was.

She trailed after the housekeeper, who led her up a grand staircase and down a corridor. They passed through a drawing room with oak paneled walls and eighteenth- century furniture. The delicate chairs with gilded arms and embroidered upholstery were exquisite. The desk, which sat at the far end of the room, was covered with books, many open, their pages reflecting the early evening sunlight. Daphne could only imagine how beautiful this room would be with the fireplace and chandelier lit.

The room was far more beautiful than her father's townhouse, and yet she remembered her father's pride in their little house in Mayfair. She could still see his face as they entered the white painted entryway for the first time. She'd just turned fourteen and the thrill of living among titled peers and wealthy aristocrats had been exciting. It had been her father's dream for years to live in that part of London.

"She's beautiful, eh? We shall certainly fit in here, won't we?" Her father's brown eyes had twinkled merrily.

If only she had known how desperate he would become,

trying to maintain that way of life, that he would destroy them both.

Daphne paused behind Mrs. Stewart as the housekeeper unlocked the bedroom door and smiled at her.

"In here, miss. This is the blue room."

Daphne entered and glanced around. The bedroom had robin's egg blue walls and a bright walnut, four poster bed. Framed watercolor sketches of Highland wildflowers hung on every wall. The warmth of the room was both feminine and welcoming.

"Once you and his lordship are wed, we shall move you to the chambers for the Countess of Huntley in the opposite wing. I'll have the footmen fill your bath. Do you have luggage?" Mrs. Stewart was now surveying her closely, and Daphne had to swallow the sudden lump in her throat.

"She doesn't have any clothes, Mrs. Stewart," Lachlan said from behind her, making both ladies jump. "Mrs. Stewart, tomorrow, be so kind as to fetch the modiste from the village. I wish to have Miss Westfall fit for clothes. You might as well make inquiries about finding her a lady's maid, as well, unless one of the upstairs maids will do?"

"We do have Mary. We can spare her if you wish to elevate her to a lady's maid," Mrs. Stewart said.

"That will be acceptable," Lachlan replied, then glanced at Daphne. "Mrs. Stewart, you may return to your duties. I should like a moment alone with Miss Westfall."

Daphne wrung her hands as the housekeeper left. Lachlan closed the bedroom door. They were alone in a bedroom, which shouldn't have worried her. They were engaged, after all, and she had slept with him in a hay loft, yet this felt more...scandalous.

"We have to have a story," he said quietly.

She tried not to appear restless under his intense stare. "A story?" she echoed.

"Aye. How we met. I meant to discuss this with you in private before we arrived, but I've been distracted these last two days. My mother will not approve if she thinks we met at an auction."

"Oh...yes. I understand." Daphne relaxed a little. "Perhaps we ought to stick to the truth as close as we can? You met me through Anthony, a mutual friend. You heard I fell on troubled times, you thought marriage might be beneficial to us both."

Lachlan placed his hands on his hips as his gaze roamed the lovely room, looking anywhere but at her.

"Aye, that might work, but my mother will be surprised I did not marry for love."

At this Daphne had nothing to say. She too had wanted to marry for love, yet here they were, no love between them.

"Then tell her the truth, that you rescued me from the streets. I can bear the shame of my situation, if it eases your mind."

He spun to face her. "Why must you always do that?"

"Do what?"

"Accept the shame of your condition? You never fight, lass, you simply..." He made a frustrated noise and raked a hand through his hair.

"Never fight?" she whispered. Her body vibrated with anger. "I have fought, Lord Huntley. I fought every day to keep myself clothed and to find a dry place to sleep. I begged every friend for work, I tried to find any employment I could, but..." Her voice trailed off.

"But what?"

"But my father committed a terrible crime, and was punished for it. The reach of his ruination went deep. Not even the street sweepers would take me on."

A pause filled the air between them, and when Daphne spoke next, it was with a heavy air that almost dragged her to the floor. "I am *tired,* Lord Huntley. I am tired of fighting. When you rescued me, I thought...I thought perhaps I might have a moment of happiness, that I might have a home. And if not that, then perhaps a little peace. If I have caused you trouble, if I am not the woman you imagined I would be, then why not send me away?"

Daphne began to tug at the gown she wore, desperate to be free of it and everything else that did not belong to her. She'd made a grave mistake in agreeing to marry a stranger. She wasn't going to stand here and take any more of his judgment when he didn't know what it was like to starve and beg.

Just then, his hands clasped her face and tilted her head back. She had only a glimpse of the emotions that warred upon his face before he lowered his head and kissed her.

Lachlan's mouth moved over hers, bruising her with his intensity, yet she welcomed the passion. The blaze of heat that flowed between them left her dizzy and she curled her arms around his neck. She'd never been kissed before, but it felt wonderful, terrifying in a way, but absolutely *wonderful.* One of his hands fisted in her hair at the nape of her neck and the other gripped her hip possessively as he pulled her closer.

"God, you taste sweet," he murmured between kisses. Daphne threaded her fingers through his hair, tugging on the strands as her body pulsed with a sudden awareness of Lachlan's strength. He was so much taller. His strong arms could so easily harm her, but they held her gently, firmly, and he kissed her until she felt faint. It made her think of the first time she drank a glass of sherry—the delightful buzz, the warm tingling that flowed through her body, but there was something else, a sharp pain deep in her womb.

She rocked her hips, needing to be closer. "Lachlan, I feel..."

"I know, lass." He lowered his lips to her neck and nipped

her shoulder, which sent fiery tingles down her spine. His fingers played with the buttons of her gown and she couldn't help but giggle. It was the first time in so long that she'd laughed.

The sound broke through whatever wildness seemed to hold him and his hands dropped from her body. He stepped back and the distance between them became a chasm.

"Apologies. That was presumptuous of me. Dinner is in one hour." His tone was polite but distant.

She nodded, her heart now aching from his sudden coldness.

"Very good. I'll fetch you then. I'll have a maid find you something to wear this evening. The modiste will come tomorrow to fit you for some proper clothes." He didn't meet her eyes as he spoke, and his hands were curled into fists at his sides.

Was he angry? Why? What could she have done to upset him? Daphne bit her lip as she watched him leave. She'd never met a man so determined to walk away from her.

She collapsed onto the bed and stroked the blue satin coverlet as she tried not to cry.

He isn't worth your tears, the voice inside her insisted, but it didn't prevent the prick of those treacherous tears. She reached into the pocket of her gown and felt for the pearls, relieved as the silken beads slid between her fingers.

For a long moment, she didn't move as she studied the beautiful blue room and the single tapestry hanging behind the headboard of the bed. A unicorn was encased in a circular fence with maidens dancing around it. The scene of the ladies in the forest with the unicorn teased her imagination and her longing. Her mother had loved to tell her stories about maidens fair and unicorns as pure white as snow. The ache in her heart grew deeper, pulsing like an old wound struck anew.

I don't deserve to be here, not after what father did.

The thought filled her with a sinking uncertainty. Could she handle being the Countess of Huntley? Could she handle living with Lachlan? What had she agreed to by coming here and marrying him? Lachlan's behavior baffled her. One minute he was furious, the next he was cold, and the next he was kissing her until she grew dizzy and breathless.

Could she really marry a man whose moods changed so unexpectedly? Then again, what choice did she have? If she broke the contract, she would be sent back to London. The contracted money wouldn't last forever. Perhaps Lachlan's mercurial moods would settle once they married.

She could only hope that would be the case.

A knock came at the door and she glanced up, expecting to see Lachlan, hoping for a chance to speak to him and try to fix whatever had gone wrong at the end of their kiss. Her heart sank as a young maid of perhaps sixteen or seventeen entered the room. Her arms were full of clothes, which she set on the bed.

"Afternoon miss, my name is Mary. I'm to help you while you are here. I've been properly trained as a lady's maid." The girl was bright-eyed and quick to smile, but blushed when she did so.

"Thank you, Mary." Daphne returned the girl's smile.

Mary began setting brushes and hair pins out on the vanity table. It reminded her of home. She missed Eugenia, her maid. When her father had been convicted, she had been evicted from the townhouse, she had urged the few remaining loyal servants to seek new employers for she could no longer pay them. Eugenia had pleaded to stay with her, but Daphne couldn't hurt one of her few remaining friends by dragging her down too. If Eugenia had stayed with her, they both would have ended up on the streets without work. It was better for Eugenia to find a new lady to serve.

"I brought fresh clothes for you." Mary walked over to the

bed and held up a simple, dark blue walking dress and the necessary undergarments. "I know they aren't much, but we are similar in size and they will do until the modiste arrives. Mrs. Marchby usually has quite a few gowns ready-made that she can adjust to fit most ladies who need something quickly. Should I call for a hot bath?"

"Yes, please." Daphne was looking forward to soaking in a tub. She'd only had the chance to bathe once at Anthony's, and she was desperate to do so again.

Mary pulled the bell cord by the bed, then set about retrieving fresh bed linens from the dressers.

"Mary, could you tell me more about the house and the servants? I should like to know as much as possible about my new home."

"Of course, miss." Mary's delighted smile and happy tales about life on the estate eased Daphne's weary heart. Huntley Castle sounded like a wonderful place to live. She only hoped Lachlan would not regret bringing her here.

Daphne and the maid spoke in whispers as footmen carried in buckets of hot water and filled the copper tub in the dressing room. The young men glanced their way, trying to hide their smiles.

Mary finally intervened. "Off with you now! She's got plenty of water." One of the young men dared to steal a kiss from Mary when he thought Daphne wasn't watching. But she saw the tender scene reflected in the mirror and smiled. Maybe someday she and Lachlan would be that spontaneous, feel that sort of love, and steal kisses when they thought no one was watching. If the kiss they'd shared a short while ago had been a bonfire, his kisses would warm her through the coldest winters, burning through the dark and healing her heart.

"Ready, miss?" Mary returned and helped her out of her clothes.

When Daphne was undressed, she stood naked in the dressing room, clutching the pearls to her chest. Where could she put them and feel confident that they would not be lost? Mary didn't miss her possessive hold over the necklace.

"Shall I find a small box to store those in for you, my lady?"

The word *no* was on the tip of her tongue, but this was her new home and she had to make herself comfortable here. Being able to leave her mother's pearls somewhere safe during the day would be necessary.

"That would be nice. Thank you."

"Of course." The maid smiled and carefully collected the pearls from Daphne's hands, then left her alone to bathe.

Daphne sank into the large copper tub, allowing the hot water to slip over her skin, its warmth sinking deep into her tired muscles. The hot water reminded her of being wrapped in Lachlan's arms, how he'd held her close in the hay, his body heat warming her. A tremor shook her and the spot between her thighs pulsed with a sharp ache. His lips had pressed into her hair...hair that now hung damp against her neck. Daphne reached up and touched the locks, feeling once again his lips so close to her neck, wishing she could feel more of his delicious, forbidden heat.

Last night in the stables, she had felt warm and safe. But then, any place was preferable to London's icy alleys. She had woken once during the night to find Lachlan curled against her, his lips buried in her hair, his hands both possessive and tender as he held her. Whatever plagued him during the day seemed to vanish at night. His worry-creased brows had softened and for a moment she had a chance to admire his masculine beauty. His full lips, lips she now knew to be soft and hot, had looked so inviting. His proud aristocratic features seemed to be chiseled out of marble.

If only I could understand him and his changing moods.

His older brother's death had to play some part in it. She understood that kind of heartbreak. Losing her mother to a weak heart, her father to prison, and her security to the courts, she'd had her heart broken over and over again. Lachlan had clearly been close to his brother and losing him... that could break even the strongest man. It was understandable for him to be rough and unfeeling when he was protecting his heart, but Daphne wished he knew he didn't have to guard against her. They could band together in their grief and become stronger for their union. She just had to make him see that.

After she finished her bath, Mary helped her dress. Luckily, the maid was right, they were close in size, and the plain white stockings and sensible, dark blue gown fit well enough. Mary handed her a lovely red and green tartan shawl.

"'Tis the family colors, my lady. I thought his lordship would like to see you wearing it tonight at dinner." Then Mary held up a rosewood box. "I've put your pearls inside, and if you leave the box on your vanity table it will be untouched." The maid set the box in Daphne's hands and Daphne couldn't resist peeking in to see that her mother's necklace lay safety inside the black velvet interior of the box.

Her throat tightened. "Thank you, Mary. I'm sorry I acted so silly, but they were my mother's and I would..." She swallowed past the lump in her throat. "They are all I have left of her."

"I understand, miss," the maid assured her before heading to the dressing room.

Daphne turned away to hide her embarrassment and to set the box on the dark brown vanity table beside the bay window. For a moment. she gazed at the box, remembering how her mother used to twine the pearls around her fingers as she dressed for dinner. Daphne's father would then enter the room and smile.

"How's my two beautiful girls?" he'd ask and then he would take the pearls and fasten them around Daphne's mother's neck and kiss her cheek, making her blush. It had been a romantic sight that Daphne, as a little girl, had safely locked away in her heart. Papa as he had been before they lost her mother and before he ruined her life.

"Are you ready for dinner?" Lachlan's voice came from the doorway. She jumped yet again. That man had the worst habit of sneaking up on her. She hadn't even heard the door open.

"I'm as ready as I'll ever be." She tried to smile at him as his cool gaze swept over her.

"You look acceptable." He crooked his arm and she slid her hand through his arm, relief fluttering through her. Was he finally playing the part of a gentleman now that they were in his home?

"Thank you," she replied a little stiffly.

She accompanied him down the corridor until they reached the grand staircase. As they descended, she brushed her fingertips over the polished banister. Huntley Castle was lovely, but would it ever feel like home? Daphne vowed at that moment she would do everything in her power to make this place somewhere she could belong. And, if she was lucky, win Lachlan's heart, as well.

5

Lachlan couldn't get the memory of that kiss out of his head. Daphne had tasted as sweet as strawberries, her soft lips utterly tempting, and her curves made for his hands. It was a miracle he managed to stop. If he hadn't heard her giggle, he might not have been able to. He would have laid her flat on the bed, her skirts tossed up over her waist and buried himself within her. He'd wanted her to clutch at his shoulders and writhe in ecstasy. The old Lachlan would have reveled in such reactions. Knowing a man could give pleasure to a woman so fully that she lost her control and sense of self had been one of his joys in life.

But that laugh of delight had been a douse of cold water. It shocked him from his haze of lust and, for that, he was grateful. Marrying her wasn't supposed to be about making her happy or giving her pleasure. It was about justice. It was about revenge. It was about *William*. He could not dishonor his brother's memory by becoming distracted by her. Oh, he would bed the pretty lass and likely enjoy it, but he was not going to allow her to have a happy life here. Her marriage would be penance for William's death.

"You're scowling again," Daphne whispered as they entered the large dining room.

Lachlan tried to ignore how delectable she looked, even in a simple servant's day gown and a tartan shawl wrapped around her shoulders. Freshly bathed, her hair smelling sweet and her skin glowing, she looked too innocent, too good to be Richard Westfall's daughter. If only she wasn't... If only.

"I'm not scowling," he muttered.

"You are..." she said in that sweet voice. He was tempted to smile, but his mother waited for them, drawing his attention to other matters. They must have looked like a happily affianced couple, their bodies close as he escorted Daphne to her chair.

"There you are, Lachlan. I wondered if you two had become distracted."

He forced a smile for her, even though it felt like a grimace.

"Come and sit by me, Miss Westfall." The Dowager Countess patted the seat beside her.

"Thank you." Daphne tried to pull free of his arm, but Lachlan escorted her all the way over to his mother and pulled back the chair for her. It gave him another chance to touch her, to brush his fingertips over her shoulders when he pushed her chair closer to the table after she was seated.

"Please, call me Daphne, my Lady."

"Then you must call me Moira." His mother beamed at Daphne. She smiled back, and for a moment Lachlan couldn't remember why he'd brought Daphne here. All thoughts of anger and vengeance were obliterated like shadows beneath a noonday sun. The open joy in her voice as she spoke to his mother was entrancing.

I shouldn't be captivated, not by her. Anyone but her... The guilt of his brother's loss prickled like an incurable itch, just out of reach.

"Lachlan, dear, when is the wedding to be?" Moira asked when he sat down across from them.

"The day after tomorrow," he replied.

His mother's brow knit with confusion. "So soon? That's hardly sufficient time to prepare."

"I need only to meet with the vicar at the Kirk of Huntley and schedule a quick service."

His mother was openly frowning now. "But your bride needs a proper trousseau."

"She doesn't require such fine things." He smiled at his mother, his tone teasing, yet as he turned to Daphne, he added a bite to his gaze. "Do you?" A spark of fire blazed in her eyes, and her lips parted in protest before she composed herself.

"Quite right. In fact, I insisted that we not make a fuss. It seems so unkind to focus on a wedding whilst the family is still in mourning for William. A quiet, simple wedding is proper."

"Really Lachlan, you must be willing to spend a little on your bride. This doesn't happen every day. I know society dictates we stop living while we mourn, but I, for one, think it is wrong. Weddings should be a happy affair and we should act accordingly. We are quite comfortable and can afford to buy her a trousseau."

He didn't miss the way Daphne shifted in her chair at the mention of money.

"If you don't wish for a trousseau for her, fine," his mother continued. "But we must still invite a few friends to the wedding."

Lachlan did not want anyone to be there, but a few witnesses would be required.

"What about Cameron McLeod and Eliza?" Moira asked. When Daphne showed open confusion, Moira patted her arm and added. "Cameron and Lachlan have been friends since they were wee bairns. They live only a short distance away. Cameron recently married. Eliza is a sweet lass."

"Oh, that would be lovely." Daphne's shoulders sagged in relief and Lachlan now frowned. He didn't want his close friends to see him marry the daughter of the man who had driven William to his death. Not that anyone except him would ever know the truth, but his victory was grim and he didn't wish to celebrate it.

"Please, Lachlan." Daphne breathing his first name drew him from the thoughts that shadowed his heart.

Candlelight illuminated her features, showing her full and beseeching eyes. That soft part of his heart he thought he'd buried with William resurrected itself.

"I should like very much to meet your friends." Her smile was tentative and shy.

He tried to cling to the edges of his anger and bitterness. *Tell her no, just say no.* But the refusal never made it past his lips.

"Er... I suppose I could invite them. We will need witnesses, after all."

"Wonderful!" Moira exclaimed. "We will make a party of it. I know we must still mourn, but I could do with a bit of laughter in this house. I believe it's what William would have wanted."

Both women turned to him, hope shining in their eyes. Lachlan knew he would never win an argument if both his mother and bride aligned. He stared down at the food as dinner was brought in, but did not think he could eat. Conversation moved around him and he felt much like a large stone cast in a stream. The rivers of words flowed around him, unstoppable, soothing. He hated how easily his mother and his fiancée got along. He threw in a word or two when questions were sent his way, but the ladies seemed content to talk on without him.

He had made the foolish assumption that by bringing Daphne here, he could control her happiness and keep her defeated and miserable. But he hadn't planned that his mother would take to Daphne so quickly. Since William's death, she'd been quiet, her heart wounded by her grief. Now he saw the glint of joy in her eyes and he welcomed the return of her smile. If he ruined Daphne's happiness, it would make his mother retreat into her pain all over again and he could not do that to her.

I should never have agreed to meet Daphne. Damn Anthony and his foolish ideas.

He could still break the contract and send Daphne back to Anthony. But Lachlan couldn't stomach the thought of another man claiming her.

He listened to his mother and Daphne talk, but the longer he watched them, the more his stomach turned to knots. He shoved his chair back and stood. Moira and Daphne turned to him, eyes wide in surprise.

"Excuse me. I'm afraid I don't feel well." He offered no other explanation, but simply left the dining room.

The corridor outside was dark, with evening shadows playing tricks upon his eyes. He paused at the base of the grand stairs to face the portrait of his older brother. William stood proud in his kilt and black coat. His face held an eerie, life-like quality. The artist had captured the hint of sorrow in his eyes and the worry lines around his mouth. William had always been one to fret over even the smallest of details.

Brother, why did you do it?

He closed his eyes. The memories were there, swirling just beneath the surface like the waters of a deep loch. He couldn't block out the past; it came rushing up to meet him, drowning him.

The late fall at Huntley Castle was always exquisite. The gardens were just beginning to lose their summer blossoms and the walkways were littered with colored petals. The trees were turning a brilliant array of reds and golds, which set the sky on fire when the sun began to set behind the edge of the castle.

Lachlan soaked in the beautiful view as he rode up to the front steps. As he dismounted, he felt that the world held out every answer, every dream to him. He smiled as he dropped the reins into the hands of the waiting groom and took a step toward the door. Out of the corner of his eye, he saw William at the window of his study, watching him. Lachlan waved, eager to see his brother. He'd only just returned from a month in London.

But William hadn't waved back. He hadn't seen Lachlan, at all. His gaze had been distant, seeing things beyond the window's view. Then he noticed the pistol in William's hand.

Why—

Lachlan rushed into the house, but he only made it a few feet before the shot rang out.

"William!" Lachlan plunged into his brother's study, skidding to a halt inside. He saw William's leg stretched out from behind his elegant desk.

"Will—" the name choked him. William didn't move.

Lachlan stumbled forward, his legs leaden and his hand shaking as he approached the desk and leaned over to stare down at the pistol laying close to William's right hand. And when he turned his gaze away, he saw the crimson splatter staining the wall.

The contents of Lachlan stomach threatened to rise. He covered his lips with the back of his hand, a strangled sound escaping his lips.

"Oh God...Oh God..."

The rustle of people in the doorway shocked Lachlan back to life. He felt as though he'd been split down the middle, like a lightning strike hitting an old oak tree. Part of him, the carefree part, was gone. What remained was a shell. That part of him took charge, sending a footman for the doctor, even though William was clearly gone. He ordered his mother to be kept away. She couldn't be allowed to see her son like this.

How long he stood there as the world passed around and by him, he wasn't sure. The body was covered and taken away, blood wiped from the walls. Only the dark, almost black, stain on the carpet remained.

Lachlan's knees shook as he collapsed into William's desk chair. His eyes burned as he fought to breathe past the agony that ripped through him like a storm upon the coast. He struggled to suck in a painful breath as he stared at his brother's desk.

That was when he'd seen the letter. Neatly written in William's hand, the quill placed at the bottom of the page. The remaining ink had dripped down to form a tiny black pool beneath his signature.

MOTHER,

I am sorry for all the pain my passing will cause you and Lachlan. I cannot bear the shame I have brought upon myself. In the coming days, you will learn of my involvement with a man named Richard Westfall. He was an investor I foolishly trusted with some measure of our family fortune. I assure you that we have not lost enough to ruin us, but Richard has been arrested for crimes of counterfeiting banknotes. He was using his notes to payout returns to his investors. I have accepted and used these funds and I encouraged many men I trusted to invest with him, who lost everything because of me. The guilt and shame of my involvement is too much to bear. I was never the man to run Huntley. That burden now falls to Lachlan. No doubt he will prove to be a better son than I ever was. Please pray for my damned soul. I hope I shall someday have the peace that I was deprived of in life.

Yours always,
William

Lachlan took the letter and locked it in the desk drawer. His mother could never be allowed to read it, yet he could not bring himself to burn the letter. Their mother would be devastated to learn the depths of William's struggle to find peace within himself.

Moira would blame herself for failing to see William's despair and not intervening to save him. If he could make one good come from this nightmare, he would spare their mother that particular agony.

Lachlan pulled himself out of the past, his heart heavy and his soul empty. He stared again into the layers of oil that formed his brother's face and saw the hollow, haunted look that had rarely left his brother's face while he lived.

You left us, Will, and you made me step into your life, a life I didn't want. I cannot forgive you for this.

Lachlan closed his eyes and drew in a shaky breath, then made for the library at the far end of the house. The servants kept a fully stocked liquor cabinet in the room, and tonight he had every desire to drink himself into oblivion.

I want to forget you, Will. Forget you, forget Daphne and her warm brown eyes and petal soft lips. I want to drown it all away.

He knew the relief from his pain would be temporary, but he would do anything right now for a few blessed hours of numbness.

6

"Tell me, my dear, how did you meet Lachlan?" Moira asked after Lachlan abruptly left dinner.

Daphne struggled to compose herself lest she betray the truth of her circumstances.

"At a private dinner party hosted by Sir Anthony Heathcoat. He was very sweet to invite me. I only knew him a little." Daphne did her best to stick to the broad elements of the truth.

"And you love my son?" The hope in Moira's eyes made Daphne's heart stutter. She wanted to love Lachlan, but the man was making that more than difficult.

She swallowed hard. "I want to love him, yet I must admit, we are both still strangers in many ways."

Moira rested one elbow on the table, her dessert plate abandoned. "You still wish to marry him then?"

Using her fork, Daphne carefully played with a bit of bread pudding on her plate as she considered how best to answer. Finally, she looked directly into Moira's eyes. "Your son rescued me when I needed a friend the most. Our desire to marry was a natural course of action that stemmed from that, and I wish to be worthy of him as a wife and a friend." Daphne meant every word. He had saved her from life in a brothel. The least she could do was make their marriage a good one, and perhaps banish whatever demons seemed to haunt Lachlan.

"Lachlan never ceases to surprise me." Moira gave a soft laugh, rich with amusement. "He was the more stubborn of my boys. The lover, the fighter, the one who broke the rules more often than not. I always believed he would wait forever before marrying." A flash of melancholy crossed her face before she offered Daphne a wry smile. "I assumed William would marry first. He was always so conscious of his duty to the estate."

"What was his brother like? Lachlan hasn't spoken of him." Daphne tried to still her racing heart, but she wanted to know more about Lachlan's family.

Moira appeared surprised. "William? He hasn't told you?"

Daphne shook her head.

Moira's pale blue eyes filled with tears and sorrow tempered her smile.

"William was my firstborn. You never forget your first bairn. I thought my body would break apart when he came into this world. He was such a quiet, wee lad. He was smart and kind, but there was a sadness to him as well. Do you know what I mean?"

Daphne's throat tightened. "Yes, I do." She'd had a friend once, a lovely girl from a good family, but no matter how warm the sunshine or how lovely the day, the girl was always... perhaps sad was the wrong word. Maybe, unaffected by the world, for good or ill.

"And Lachlan? What was he like as a boy?"

"Lachlan was my little warrior, fit for the clans of old. There were always biscuits to steal, trees to climb. He was fearless. But I grow concerned that something changed with

William's passing." Moira blushed. "I cannot explain it, but the light in his eyes seems dimmer." She reached out and touched Daphne's cheek in a motherly caress. "Except now, for just a moment, when he watched you laugh, I saw a glint of the old spirit in his eyes. Mayhaps this marriage will be a good thing for you both."

Daphne's heart raced at the thought of her laughter having that effect on Lachlan. For two months she had felt so helpless, so useless, but now she had a chance to help someone.

"I know he doesn't seem to care about your trousseau, but I was thinking you might fit into my wedding gown. It's a bit old in style, but I believe I was about your size when I wore it. We can have the modiste make the necessary alterations, of course."

Her heart swelled and she had to resist the urge to hug Lachlan's mother. "Thank you, I would be honored."

"I think, my dear, it is time I retire for the evening. I'm not so young as I once was." She smiled again. "You know the way back to your room?"

"Yes, I'll be fine."

She and Moira rose from the table and parted ways. For a long moment, Daphne stood in the dim corridor, thinking of Lachlan and his brother. When she began walking again, she sought out the main stairs, but paused at the sight of a portrait she'd missed earlier that day. The morning sunlight had favored the stairs, leaving the walls in shadow and she hadn't looked closely. Yet now, moonlight basked the portraits on the wall with a milky light. The face staring back at her was unmistakable.

It had to be William. The clothing was modern, and his features were so much like Lachlan's. Yet she saw an eternal melancholy in his eyes, just as Moira had described.

"He was a good man, my brother." Lachlan's slightly slurred voice came from the shadows by the entryway straight ahead of her. Daphne bit her lip to keep from gasping and her stomach churned with a deep uneasiness. Lachlan had an obvious talent for sneaking up on her when she least expected him.

"Your mother told me a little about him," Daphne admitted.

Lachlan emerged from the shadows, his tall body imposing in the darkness. She had the sudden image of him overpowering her, catching hold of her body and kissing her, uncaring of whether she wished him to or not. His waistcoat was gone and he held a bottle of Scotch in one hand. His cravat was missing and his hair was tousled, as though he had run his hand through it repeatedly.

"And did she tell you how he died?" His voice was soft, but Daphne sensed danger in the question. He turned away from her and she thought for a moment he'd forgotten her, lost in memories.

"Er...no, she didn't."

He spun to face her and stepped closer, the contents of his bottle swishing in the silence of the house.

"He took his own life." Lachlan stood only a few feet away now. She inhaled the heavy perfume of Scotch as it rolled off him. He'd been drinking too much. She shouldn't stay alone with him, not when he was in such a condition.

"My lord, perhaps I should fetch someone to—"

He caught her arm, firmly but gently, and kept her close to him, caged by his body.

"No need to get anyone. I've been deeper in my cups than this." He chuckled. "Do I frighten you?"

She gazed into his eyes, searching for any aggression or brutality. She saw only sorrow and curiosity.

"Frighten me? No," she finally replied.

"Good." He set the bottle down on the foot of the stairs and placed one hand on the banister, trapping her against it.

She leaned back, the wood railing pressing into her spine until she could not retreat any farther. He reached for her hip, his fingers curling into the loose fabric of her gown, as he secured a firm hold.

"And now?"

Daphne's blood pounded in her head and she felt suddenly dizzy. "Only a little."

She raised her chin as he tilted his head slightly. His lips, so often curved in a frown, twitched as though tempted to smile.

"I'd never hurt you, lass." He lowered his head, giving her plenty of time to resist, to push him away, but she didn't want to. Their mouths met in a slow kiss that burned like a warm fire. She tasted the Scotch on his lips and was lost in the headiness it created within her. She had forgotten what it felt like to be warm, to feel a fire obliterate the cold inside of her.

She curled her arms around his neck, pulling him closer, needing more of his touch, and his heat. When he kissed her, she felt like she was falling, breathless and free, into a world where the past no longer mattered. Only this moment existed, the brush of soft lips and sweet sighs...

"What are you doing to me?" he demanded in a panting whisper between kisses.

I'm loving you. The thought rose unbidden to answer him and it startled her. She barely knew Lachlan, but it was true, she *wanted* to love him, was even at this moment falling in love with him.

He reached up and cupped her face, their eyes meeting briefly before he deepened the kiss once more, and plundered her mouth in the most sinful way. Daphne moaned as ripples of fire stirred throughout her body. She couldn't resist threading her fingers through his dark hair, tugging on the silken strands. He growled against her lips and used one hand to drag her skirts up to her waist.

He gripped the back of her left thigh and lifted her leg up to crawl around his hip. Daphne didn't fully understand what he wanted her to do, but her primal instincts took over and she rocked against him. To her delight, she found the hard press of his muscled thigh against the apex of hers, intense and overpowering. Sensations shot through her from the simple but intense friction. Lachlan leaned against the banister, his thigh rubbing harder against her sensitive mound through the thin layers of her underclothes.

"Ride me," he murmured, showing her the natural rhythm of their bodies moving together.

Once she matched it, it was too much to bear. His tongue played with hers and her breasts ached against her stays as he assaulted her every sense. His taste, the hint of Scotch, the smell of leather and man mixed with his rough caress and the sting of his hand fisting in her hair as he began to kiss her ruthlessly. He was conquering her with every weapon at his disposal and she was more than ready to surrender. If he had wanted to take her there on the stairs, she would have let him.

The building pressure and the dark need for some kind of release became unbearable. She whimpered as he rubbed his thigh over and over against her mound. Then he suddenly changed direction, rolling his hips in a slightly different direction, and the explosive release of a frightening pleasure was unbearable. Daphne cried out against his lips and he pulled away from her with a curse. The abrupt separation made her stumble on the steps. She barely caught herself against the banister before she fell.

Without a word, much less an explanation, Lachlan started up the stairs, leaving her alone, legs shaking and body aching with a loss she didn't understand. How could he have touched her so intimately, so... She blinked back tears. He'd roused deep feelings within her, not simply passion, and then he'd left her alone, cold and confused. The evening sunset had faded an hour ago, leaving soft purple beams of moonlight painting the walls with a melancholy splash of color.

Daphne stared up at the portrait of Lachlan's brother and shivered. His pained eyes seem to gaze right through her.

"What am I supposed to do?" she asked him in a barely audible whisper.

The handsome, tragic man in the portrait offered no reply, leaving Daphne feeling more alone than she'd ever felt before.

"YOU'RE GETTING MARRIED?" CAMERON MCLEOD BURST out laughing.

"It's not amusing," Lachlan barked. He glared at his best friend. Cameron couldn't seem to stop grinning and was barely restraining himself. Laughs still escaped as snorts and hisses, which made him sound one gasp away from giggling like a girl.

"For heaven's sake," Lachlan punched his shoulder in only a partially playful manner, but Cameron's good-natured grin didn't fade. His eyes were alight with mischief.

"Well, don't go silent on me, Lachlan. Describe this paragon of a girl who has captured your heart."

"She hasn't," he replied. She'd captured his interest, his arousal, but not his heart.

At this, Cameron sobered immediately. "You...you don't love this lass you're planning to marry? But you always swore you wouldn't marry, not unless you fell madly in love."

Cameron frowned as he and Lachlan strode toward the small stone church. The Kirk of Huntley was a quaint Gothic structure that had been around for hundreds of years and would likely be there long after he was dust. He paused as he reached a heavy oak door and grasped the handle, unable to look his friend in the eye.

"That was before I became an earl. I have a duty to marry and provide for an heir." The words tasted like poison. Marrying out of duty was bad enough, but marrying for revenge was worse, yet here he was intending to do just that.

Cameron placed his hand on the church door, preventing Lachlan from opening it. "Do you even *like* your future bride?"

"I like her well enough. She's fetching and sweet."

Cameron rolled his eyes, but his gaze was serious when he finally lifted his hand from the door.

"'Marrying for anything other than love is damned foolish.' Those are your words, Lachlan."

Lachlan exhaled slowly, closing his eyes for a brief moment. "Losing William has made me stop thinking like a foolish and unrealistic child. It's time I settled down with one woman and made the best of it. If you do not approve, you don't have to witness tomorrow's wedding."

"Not come? I wouldn't miss it. I only want you happy." Cameron followed him into the church, their voices lowered out of respect as they walked down the aisle. The echo of their boots on the stone floor summoned the vicar, John McKenzie. Lachlan greeted the middle-aged vicar and shook his hand.

"My lord, what service can I do for you?" The vicar's bright blue eyes appeared amplified behind the spectacles perched on his nose.

"A wedding. I need a wedding tomorrow."

"Oh? And who's the lucky man?" John glanced at Cameron and chuckled. "I seem to recall marrying you only last month."

Cameron laughed and pointed a thumb in Lachlan's direction. "It's him, if you can believe it."

McKenzie blinked in surprise. “You, my Lord?”

“Why is everyone so shocked that I am to be married?”

John smiled. “Hardly a year ago, you said you would never marry, not unless someone made you.” The humor faded from his eyes. “There isn’t a...reason that a ceremony is required in such short time, is there? You know how I—”

“No,” Lachlan couldn’t keep the sarcasm out of his voice. “The lass still clings to her precious maidenhead. I simply want the wedding to be done quickly.” Lachlan didn’t care for their assumptions, and had grown tired of everyone questioning his motives. That the truth was far worse, didn’t help matters.

The minister pursed his lips and, after exchanging a glance with Cameron, shrugged.

“And what’s the lucky lass’s name? Is she from this area?”

“No. She’s English.”

Both Cameron and McKenzie stared at him.

“You’re bringing a Sassenach to live here? With you?” Cameron started laughing again.

“There’s a bit of a problem with her residency,” McKenzie replied more seriously, “and the banns...”

“Aye, I figured as much.” Lachlan glanced around the church, noting some of the wooden rafters were a bit fractured. “And what of your church? Perhaps a bit of timber could find its way here?”

McKenzie glanced up at the same rotted timbers. “I suppose the banns can be read today three times and...well, we could have the church ready for a ceremony tomorrow at nine in the morning. Does that suit you, my lord?”

“Aye, that does.” Lachlan glanced once more at the stained-glass windows and the kaleidoscope of pale colors cast over the wooden pews.

“And this is to be a private affair?” John asked.

Lachlan finally faced the minister again, expecting more questions. "Yes. Cameron and Eliza will witness."

"Very well. Is that all you need, my lord?"

"Yes, that is all." He and Cameron bid the minister farewell and then they exited the church.

"Cameron, why don't you bring Eliza up to Huntley Castle for a few days? Mother thinks it would cheer Daphne." He wasn't too keen on doing anything that would cheer his future wife, but it would cheer him, which was something he desperately needed. The anger he'd clung to for so long was waning and he was filled with an empty loneliness that he couldn't seem to escape. Having Cameron around for a few days would remind him of the happy man he'd once been, before Willian's death. He wanted Daphne to see him as he used to be, the man who might have fallen in love with her under different circumstances.

"I'm sure Eliza would be thrilled, and it will give me a chance to meet this woman and see if I can figure out why she has you twisted up in knots."

"I'm not twisted up in knots."

"So you say. But never in my life have I seen you so boorish. Growling like a wounded bear one minute and snapping your jaws like a wolf the next."

"McLeod..." he warned, and inwardly cursed at how the name escaped his lips in a clear growl.

"Ack, now I've done it. You're calling me McLeod." Cameron feigned distress as they reached their mounts, tied up outside the church yard.

"Be there tonight for dinner," Lachlan said as he and Cameron climbed into their saddles. His horse shifted and snorted. With a light smack on the gelding's neck, Lachlan gripped his reins and readied to leave.

"Tonight, it is." Cameron nodded to him and rode off, his home being only a few miles away.

Lachlan began the quick journey back home, wishing the distance was greater. He wasn't yet ready to face Daphne. Not after last night. He had groped her like a randy lad and she had purred like a cat in response, something he hadn't expected. The startled look of pleasure in her eyes told him she had never climaxed before. She wasn't simply a virgin, she was completely uneducated in the ways of pleasure. He tried to bury the heavy guilt he felt, knowing he would enjoy giving those lessons.

I shouldn't enjoy her, not anything about her, yet I do. It felt like a betrayal of William's memory.

For the next half hour, he was lost in thoughts of Daphne as he rode home.

As he approached the castle's entrance, he spotted a feminine figure kneeling among the rose bushes. There were no buds to admire, though, only frost on the remaining greenery. Intrigued, he rode closer, wondering if one of the maids was out...but then he recognized Daphne.

He took a moment to admire her. She worked a small pair of clippers in her gloved hands to cut a bit of a rosebush, then lifted the stem close to examine it.

"What are you doing?"

"My lord!" She gasped in shock and leapt to her feet before she spun around, her cheeks flushing. "I was retrieving a stem of this rose. I thought I might grow it inside the hothouse I discovered behind the castle."

"The hothouse? That place hasn't been tended to in years." He slid off his horse and patted its flank as he waited for Daphne to join him. She wasn't wearing a cloak, only a thin shawl, yet she seemed unbothered by the chill.

"Where's your cloak?" he asked sharply.

Daphne's face was still red. "I don't have one."

"But the modiste came today to bring you clothes." He

had seen to that personally before he'd ridden off to seek out Cameron.

"She gave me plenty of ready-made dresses and other necessary things, but she did not have a completed cloak."

"Oh..." He felt like a horse's arse for snapping at her. Lachlan stripped off his great cloak and hung it over her shoulders, noting that it pooled on the ground like a black train. He wanted her unhappy. He didn't want her catching cold and becoming ill.

"Really, my lord..."

"Lachlan. Please call me Lachlan. As your future husband, I must see to your care. That includes giving you a cloak when you are cold." He took his time, making sure it fastened securely beneath her chin. She trembled at his touch and clutched the frozen branch to her chest like a talisman.

"I thought you said you did not fear me," he whispered, stepping forward until their bodies pressed. He couldn't resist her, not when he thought of last night--the way she felt so perfect in his arms, and the way she reacted to him. The tension between them built as she raised her eyes to his.

"I don't fear *you*..." Her admission only deepened the blush staining her cheeks.

He brushed his gloved hands down the pale column of her throat. "Then what do you fear?"

"I fear how you make me feel." Her brown eyes, the color of a doe's and just as frightened, glanced away from him.

"You should never be afraid of passion. Sometimes, when all else has been stripped away, it's the only thing you have left in life," he murmured, and the truth of the words hit him deep. Passion was all he had left. Love and trust, faith, hope...all of these had perished when William died.

"You have more than that, I've seen it in your eyes. Passion is a spark, and a spark dies quickly unless it has fuel to sustain it." Daphne's eyes softened and her lips curved in a smile so full of hope that it made his heart bleed for the past.

She reached with her free hand and stroked his cheek, then cupped his face and stood up on tiptoes. She pressed her mouth to his in a way that sent his senses spinning like no chaste kiss should. He took in the fall of her thick dark lashes before he closed his eyes and returned her kiss. He realized with a stunned sense of clarity that this moment was not about passion. It was about *them*, together, their souls reaching out to one another.

He should've stopped it, but he couldn't. Kissing Daphne was like breathing. He couldn't do without her.

Lachlan tried not to think about the danger he was putting himself in by caring for the woman he planned to marry out of spite. When she finally broke away from him, she raised a hand to her mouth, touching her slightly swollen lips, which had become a lovely shade of dark pink.

"Lass..." Lachlan choked on the words he didn't want to say. "We do not have to go through with this."

She blinked, her gaze still hazy with desire. "What?"

"You don't have to marry me. I have been thinking about this and it's not fair for you to marry a stranger. I'll waive any rights to the money I set up in your trust, if that's what you're worried about."

She swallowed and spoke quietly but firmly, "I swear I didn't agree because of the money." She blushed and looked at the ground for a second. "I did need security, but after I met you and we arrived here, well, I want *this*... I want to be a part of your life. Do you wish to cry off? Is it because of something I've done?"

He placed his hands on her shoulders. "What? No!"

"Then why?"

"I'm not a good man, Daphne. I'm broken." The honesty shocked him.

"Everyone has something a little broken inside them. Perhaps our pieces fit. Don't you think we should at least try?" She bit her lip. The hard set of her face told him she wanted to marry him. The poor fool.

I tried to do the right thing. I tried.

"Perhaps we should," he agreed, fighting the temptation to kiss her again. "Let me escort you back to the house." He held out his arm and after a moment's hesitation, she slipped her arm in his. They walked side by side to the house, her with her rose branch, him leading his horse. He was struck by the strange domestic contentment of her companionship without a word needed between them.

"I met with the vicar today," he said at last.

"Oh?"

"It seems the church was in need of a bit of repair. I offered to donate timber to the parish, and Mr. McKenzie is overlooking the residency issue since you're not a resident of the Parish. He shall call out the banns three times today to satisfy the legal requirements, and then we can marry tomorrow."

"Are you sure that will be legally binding?"

"Yes. Sometimes Scottish law can be looser than English law, but do not worry, you will be the Countess of Huntley."

"I don't care about that. Titles never really mattered to me." She was smiling a little as they walked.

He shot her a sideways glance of disbelief. "Titles don't matter?"

"Not to me. My mother was the daughter of a duke, but she married down for love. I think I'm more like her than my father, at times. I care little about the *ton* and it's love of rank. It always seemed a silly thing to me."

"Oh?" He stiffened at the mention of the man who had unknowingly brought them together.

"Yes. I love my father, but he was focused on advancing

our position in society. I believe he felt he had to earn his place to make up for my mother marrying down, but he became addicted to his social climb. It was very lonely growing up with him after my mother died."

Her quiet words cut through the anger that usually filled him when that man was mentioned. But to hear about him through her eyes, the rage vanished. She, too, had lost someone she'd loved.

"How old were you when she passed?"

"I was eleven. She was fine one minute and the next, she had a bad headache. She went to sleep after tea and never woke up. It was her heart that failed, according to the doctor." She looked down at her feet. "I cried for weeks. I still miss her."

Lachlan pulled her close as he pictured her waiting for her mother to wake up, and how frightened and grief stricken she must have been when she didn't.

"I..." She hesitated as they reached the steps. She tucked her rose branch under one arm then lifted something from the pocket of her gown and held it out. When she uncurled her fingers, he saw a string of pearls coiled on her palm.

"These were my mother's. It's all I could save when the Court took my house to pay the victims of my father's crimes." Her voice wavered on the last word, but when she raised her head to look at him, fierce pride gleamed in her eyes.

"You don't wear them?" he asked, surprised at her humility.

"No. They're too precious for that. I couldn't even part with them for food and water when..." She couldn't finish her sentence.

"When you were living on the streets?" There was a time he would have taken a dark pleasure at the idea of her on the streets, cold, hungry, alone and endangered. But now the thought filled him with a hard rage, almost as suffocating as the hatred he bore for her father.

"Wear them tomorrow for the wedding," he ordered. "I want to see them on you."

"But—" she started to protest, but he placed a finger to her lips.

"*Please*. I insist. For your mother's sake. No doubt she would have wanted you to wear them."

"They won't look fetching with my plain white gown."

Regret prickled his insides, because he'd insisted that he didn't want her to have a fancy wedding trousseau.

"We could have the modiste return..."

"No," she replied. "You wanted simple, and simple I shall be." She tucked the pearls back into her gown pocket. She let go of his arm as he met a groom at the steps of the house. She did not wait for him, nor did she look his way as she entered the house alone, her head held high.

If he ever doubted she was the granddaughter of a Duke, that moment alone would've proven him wrong. And damned if the picture didn't make him smile.

7

Daphne trembled as she gazed at herself in the full-length mirror. Her new maid had helped her dress in her lovely but simple purple evening gown. Would it be good enough to please Lachlan? He'd claimed he didn't want a fancily dressed wife, but that didn't stop her from wanting to look pleasing. His friend Cameron McLeod and his new wife Eliza had arrived for dinner and Daphne couldn't shake the feeling that they would be studying her closely, measuring her to see if she made a suitable match for their friend.

"You look lovely, my lady. Truly." Mary sighed dreamily. "Purple complements your fair skin."

Daphne pressed a hand to her cheek, trying to see the beauty Mary spoke of. She had to admit, she did look...*better*. Two months of scraps had left her gaunt and feeling worn in ways she hadn't been prepared for. Having a warm bed and regular meals had been more than a relief, it had been restorative.

I am finally safe, I finally have a home.

Her eyes suddenly burned and she closed them, fighting her emotions.

Mary touched her shoulder, giving her a gentle squeeze. "My lady? Are you all right?"

She cleared her throat. "Yes. I am. 'Tis nerves, is all. I'm anxious about meeting Mr. McLeod and his wife."

Mary grinned. "There's no need to be nervous. Mr. McLeod is a perfect gentleman, especially toward the ladies. I suspect his Lordship will be the one in trouble."

"Oh?" Daphne reached for the white elbow-length gloves that had been laid out across the bed's coverlet.

"Yes, Mr. McLeod—Cameron, that is--loves to tease his Lordship. Ever since they were lads, or so I've heard. Mr. McLeod will no doubt tease him about you, as well." Mary put the brushes and extra pins into the drawers of the vanity table.

"What could he tease Lord Huntley about in regards to me?" Daphne asked.

The maid shrugged, reluctant to speak.

"Please, tell me."

Mary glanced around, as if afraid someone would hear, then said in a low voice, "It's quite well known that his Lordship has certain beliefs on marriage," she began. "He'd always proclaimed he would marry only for love. Now that he's marrying you... well, Mr. McLeod will be sure to prod him about his reasons."

"Oh dear," Daphne sighed, and a headache began to form behind her eyes.

Lachlan didn't love her and would likely be upset if his friend teased him about it.

"I wouldn't worry about it, my lady," Mary replied with a little giggle before a distant gong sounded somewhere. "Ach, dinner's ready."

Lachlan had a gong? That was unexpected. Only the finest

houses boasted such a thing. Not that Huntley Castle wasn't fine, but despite the exquisite furnishings, the estate had a rustic feel to it that made her forget she was in one of the finer houses in Scotland.

Daphne left Mary to tidy up the bedchamber. Lachlan waited for her at the bottom of the stairs, one arm resting on the newel post. The sight brought back wild, forbidden memories of last night's kiss. A kiss that had led to one of the most exquisite pleasures in her life. Her face heated and she tried to focus on anything but Lachlan and the memory of his thigh rubbing against her in that unexpected way.

"Dinner and new acquaintances," she repeated over and over until her nerves replaced the flush of arousal. She bit her lip as she reached Lachlan. He smiled, and for the first time it was warm and genuine. He held out his arm to her and she accepted his escort.

"Don't let Cameron fool you," Lachlan said as they neared the dining room. "He's quite a trickster."

"And Eliza?"

"By far, she is Cameron's better half. You will take to her, lass, do not fret."

She held her breath as they entered the dining room. Candelabras had been lit, lending a seductive glow to the long, polished dining table and the gray walls around them, which bore stately portraits of Lachlan's ancestors.

Moira stood waiting for them at the far end of the table, beaming. Firelight from the white marble hearth illuminated a couple close to Moira. The man, Cameron McLeod, was almost as tall as Lachlan, with blond hair. They dressed in similar style, but where Daphne felt they stood apart most was in their expressions. Already, she could see the trickster she had been warned about in his face. Lachlan, on the other hand, had a certain wildness about him, something that seemed untamable, and she longed to let go and be wild with him.

The woman at Cameron's side, Eliza, was a pretty woman with reddish-brown hair. She wore a fashionable gown but, like Daphne's, it was simple in cut. That came as something of a relief. The gowns from the modiste were quite good, but she feared they would not appear worthy of a countess. Of course, she was content to wear simple clothes, but at the same time, didn't want to make a poor impression and embarrass Lachlan.

"Ahh, Lachlan, you finally prove the mystery woman exists!" Cameron laughed heartily. It was an open, kind laugh, and despite the mischief that lurked there, Daphne knew she would like and trust Cameron.

Eliza poked her husband in the ribs with an elbow. "Oh, hush." She beamed at Daphne, approached, and grasped Daphne's hands.

"So lovely to meet you," Eliza said. "I'm Eliza McLeod, and this is my very silly husband, Cameron."

"It is so nice to meet you as well." Daphne couldn't stop smiling as she looked at the couple. She chanced a glance at Lachlan. He seemed more relaxed than he had ever been since they'd met.

"You look well." Moira gave Daphne a motherly hug that threatened to return burning tears to her eyes. She was suddenly ridiculously happy. She was making new friends, ones who probably didn't know about her father or her shame. She was being treated like a daughter, a fiancée and a friend.

"Shall we begin?" Lachlan asked.

Eliza and Daphne took adjacent seats at the table. Lachlan moved to its head while Cameron and Moira sat opposite Daphne and Eliza. As the courses flowed in and out of the room, Cameron regaled the diners with tales of his and Lachlan's childhood.

"...And there was the time we snuck into the bakery in the village, you remember that?" Cameron asked between sips of wine.

"I do. I also recall forbidding you from sharing that particular story," Lachlan said, his tone teasing. He leaned back in his chair, smiling. Daphne was fascinated by this change in him. He seems so at home, so alive and warm around Cameron. The ghosts of the past seemed, for now, to have been banished by their guests.

I wish I could always see him like this, smiling and happy.

Eliza snickered. "Go on, tell us what happened, Cameron."

Cameron toyed with his fork, grinning devilishly. "Well... Lachlan climbed into the back window of the bakery and started stuffing cherry tarts into his trouser pockets. But he forgot about the fat green toad we'd recently captured at the loch." He paused to let Lachlan shake his head with a rueful smile.

Daphne couldn't resist asking, "And?"

"The old baker came storming into the storeroom and saw Lachlan standing there, pockets full of tarts and me halfway out the window. He grabbed us both by our necks and gave us a good shake. Then he demanded we empty our pockets. Lachlan reaches down, pulls one out and slaps it into the man's hand. There, covered in red cherry sauce, is that toad, bug eyes wide and its throat pulsing as it croaked. The baker yelped and tossed the toad in the air. It landed on the bakery racks by the bread. Lachlan and I dove out the window and took off running before he recovered."

"I still hear that old man's bellows in my nightmares," Lachlan laughed. "If he'd ever caught us..."

"Neither of us would've been able to sit down for a

month, that much is certain," Cameron finished. "So, you see, my dear Miss Westfall, you are marrying a veritable outlaw. I hope you're prepared."

Daphne beamed at Lachlan. "Have no fear, Mr. McLeod, I shall keep the cherry tarts safely under lock and key.

"Nonsense. You need only keep plenty about for me to eat." Lachlan's casual tease felt so natural, so wonderfully sweet. It was the way she'd dreamed a husband would be with his wife. She longed for a man who would be sweet and amusing and intimate with her in all the aspects of his life. And right now, she felt that she and Lachlan had that chance.

Perhaps I might find a way to banish the ghosts in his heart the way Cameron does.

Lachlan grinned boyishly. "Enough about us, Cameron. I wish to hear Eliza play. It's been some time since anyone has used the music room."

"Eliza?" Cameron looked to his wife and she blushed and nodded.

Moira clapped her hands and stood. "Let's be off. I, too, long for some music." She joined Daphne and Eliza. "Do you play, Daphne?"

"Me? Oh... No, but I sing a little," she admitted.

"That's a good thing, for I do not," Eliza mused.

The music room was just off the dining hall. A thick, lushly carved harp sat in one corner and a pianoforte held a prominent place with several chairs facing it. A servant had thought to light a fire in the room and the candles on the two tables by the chairs were lit. Eliza seated herself at the piano, facing the small crowd over the gleaming wood of the instrument. Daphne joined her, but remained standing. A treacherous flutter of nerves made her place a hand to her stomach. Lachlan was watching her keenly, the intensity of his focus making her inwardly flounder.

"Do you know the song, *Drown it in the Bowl*?"

"Why, yes I do," Daphne said. It was a very unusual song, not one she would expect to sing in parlors, but she was happy she knew it well enough to sing while Eliza played.

"Ready?" Eliza asked.

"Yes." Daphne's voice wavered, but she cleared her throat as she listened to the notes of the piano, then closed her eyes and began to sing.

"The glossy sparkle on the board,
The wine is ruby bright,
The reign of pleasure is restor'd,
Of ease and fond delight.
The day is gone, the night's our own,
Then let us feast the soul,
If any care or pain remain,
Why drown it in the bowl."

Daphne opened her eyes and saw the open admiration of Cameron and Moira. It buoyed her spirits and she sang louder. As her gaze met Lachlan's, a shock ran through her, sizzling along her skin as she continued,

"This world they say's a world of woe,
That I do deny;
Can sorrow from the goblet flow?
Or pain from beauty's eye?
The wise are fools, with all their rules,
When they would joys control:
If life's a pain, I say again?
Let's drown it in the bowl."

She pictured the moment the officers of the law came to her house and dragged her father away; the spectators in the street who watched her eviction mere weeks after her father's sentence was announced. The cold, frightening agony and loneliness of the streets, the smooth comfort of the pearls against her fingertips, kept like a talisman against the ill will around her.

Her voice carried stronger now and she saw not only the past but a future, one she hoped to share with Lachlan. Sunny days on heather-filled meadows and nights in bed, his kisses setting fire between them.

"That time flies fast the poet sing;
Then surely it is wise,
In rosy wine to dip his wings,
And seize him as he flies.
This night is ours; then strewn with flowers
The moments as they roll:
If any pain or care remain,
Why drown it in the bowl."

Eliza played the refrain once more, then lifted her hands off the keys and laid them in her lap. Her eyes met with Daphne's and she was surprised to see the woman's eyes aglitter with tears.

"You sing beautifully," she said at last.

Daphne's throat constricted, and she looked at the small audience before her. Cameron was wide-eyed in admiration and perhaps a bit of shock, while Moira had a bittersweet smile upon her face. But Lachlan... His face was a storm of emotions.

Then, without a word, he stood and strode from the room, slamming the door behind him. Cameron exhaled a low, painful sigh before he rose and joined Daphne and Eliza.

"Eliza, why did you pick that song?" He brushed the back of his fingers over his wife's cheek. "You know it was his favorite."

"Whose favorite?" Daphne asked. "Lachlan's?"

Cameron's face turned to hers. His usual gaiety had vanished, replaced by deep grief.

"William. It was William's favorite."

"I'm sorry." Eliza stood, crossed to Moira, and hugging

her. The older woman wiped away stray tears. "I had forgotten. Please, forgive me."

"No, it was beautiful. Thank you," said Moira, then looked at the shut door. "But I fear the moment has affected poor Lachlan differently."

"I'll go talk to him," Cameron said, but Daphne caught his arm.

"Let me. I want to."

Cameron studied her. "Perhaps it would be best."

Daphne rushed from the music room and caught sight of Lachlan farther down the corridor. She followed him and realized he was headed toward the terrace. The back door to the hothouse was located near the terrace.

Lachlan entered the hothouse. Daphne slipped in behind him. The interior of the glass structure was warm, its windows fogged with moisture. A few abandoned yet blooming plants interspersed those that had withered and now stretched helplessly over dusty pot edges, their decaying vegetation filling the air with a bittersweet scent of death. Empty watering cans littered the floor, and wind whistled eerily along the windows while pale moonlight illuminated the house in creamy patches of light and shadow. She had settled her bit of rose bush here earlier in the day, having filled its pot with fresh soil.

Lachlan stood in the back of the room with one hand braced against the glass, his head bowed like a dark lord over a magical garden that slowly died around him.

"Lachlan," Daphne whispered. Her slipper trod on a dead leaf. The sharp crackle caused her to flinch. He did not move or speak.

She came up behind him, curled her arms around his waist and rested her cheek against his back. He tensed but did not pull away.

"Tell me about him."

After a long moment, he relaxed. The sigh that escaped him held a century of pain. "My brother was a good man," Lachlan said, "but plagued with sorrow. All of his life, a shadow hung inside him. No matter how bright the day or how pretty the girl smiling at him, he never..." The words roughened in his voice and she held him tighter. "He never saw the good. You understand?"

"I do." She rubbed his stomach with one hand. He reached up to take her hand and held it for a long moment. The simple connection seemed to root her, giving her hope that she could grow here beside him, two well-tended plants, twining their hearts together as plants would their roots.

"I never knew what to say to banish those clouds. I loved him fiercely, but my love was not enough."

He thought his love wasn't enough to save his brother? No wonder Lachlan and his mother suffered such pain. An accident was unexpected, but suicide... There was a helplessness to people who lost loved ones this way.

"What happened to him was not your fault," she said. "Your love was enough, but sometimes sadness is too much to bear, and it comes from deep wells that are of no one's making. It doesn't mean they do not love, do not care." She remembered all too clearly the young woman whose family had cared about her, but she too had taken her life by plunging into the Thames one night and perished. "Focus on his *life*, not his death. Times when he knew and felt your love for him. Those are the memories you must burn into your heart. Only light can banish shadows."

Only love can banish sorrow... Daphne held him, willing Lachlan to feel her heart speaking to his, to feel her love. *I want to love you. Let me. Let me help you heal.*

He turned to face her, but she didn't let go. When he looked into her eyes, she saw a glimmer on his cheeks where tears had run down his face.

"You're not at all what I expected. Not what I wanted," he murmured as he cradled her face in his hands.

"Not what you wanted?" The words hurt, but he suddenly smiled, though it was tinged with melancholy.

"No, you're far *better*. I don't believe I will ever deserve to have you as my wife."

She relaxed and smiled back. "Lucky for you, I'm bought and paid for. I'm all yours."

His hoarse chuckle tickled her ears as he leaned down and placed a soft, lingering kiss upon her lips. With that kiss, she was pulled deeper into him, this beautiful wild Scotsman with his broken heart that called to her own. He kissed her slowly, wrapping her in his strength and warmth until every worry and every fear she had faded away. There was only this moment.

Tomorrow, this wonderful man will be my husband. Tomorrow...

8

Lachlan stood at the entrance to the church, his black breeches and black waistcoat accented with gold embroidery. A red and green tartan sash was pinned at his chest with his father's brooch, which bore the Huntley seal. Beside him, Cameron stood unusually silent. A faint breeze rustled the dead leaves that were covered in frost, making the leaves look like shards of ice dancing between the tombstones when morning light illuminated them.

The castle's coach arrived and stopped at the end of the cobblestone path that led to him and the church behind him. He held his breath as the coach door opened. Eliza and his mother emerged, both smiling broadly before they stepped aside.

From the darkness of the coach, a slender hand appeared on the frame of the door. Then a dainty foot in an elegant white shoe took its first step outside. His breath caught and his chest tightened. Daphne exited the coach, the fullness of her gown now filling the doorway. He swallowed hard as she stepped to the ground. The pale crème lace netting over the white skirts was old-fashioned, but the silver threading in the shape of swans on her pale blue bodice was exquisite.

His mother caught his eye and smiled again. He recognized the gown as his mother's wedding dress.

Daphne looked like a fairy queen. Her dark hair, bronzed by the light, flashed with hints of auburn and gold. How had he not noticed that her hair was more than simply dark? Daphne lifted her head and their gazes locked. She reached up, her fingertips touching the pearls around her neck. Emotion flooded him, blinding him with an intense inner light and heat that stole his breath and stopped his heart.

The vulnerability in her gaze was overshadowed by a trust so deep he knew he could never hurt this woman, *never* betray her. Whatever his reasons for bidding on her that night at the marriage auction no longer mattered. She was to be his wife, his partner in life. He would seek her counsel, seek her love and support. It was what he always longed for, even as a foolish young lad. Love had always been his dream.

Now I have it, at a terrible cost. Indeed, had he not lost his brother, had he not been driven by vengeance, he never would have met her—and she, in turn, never would have saved him. *I have been rewarded with a priceless prize.*

Daphne lifted her skirt and started down the gravel path. The sun lit glints of silver on her gown so she glowed and sparkled like a gemstone. He'd never been one for angels and God, at least, in the literal sense, but in that moment, as he watched her approach, he *believed* in something better, something wondrous and endless. It made him feel small, yet connected to everything around him—the wind in the trees, the stones collecting moss by the road, even the chatter of the larks in the heather. For two long months, he'd barely lived, his grief so strong, it threatened to drown him. But seeing Daphne coming toward him, hope shining her eyes, he breathed again for the first time in ages. His gratitude, his affection for her, was overpowering.

When his bride reached him, he raised her hand to his lips and knelt on the ground on one knee, then bowed his head, sending a silent prayer to the heavens that he would never lose her, his precious pearl. All his anger, all his sorrow had been banished by her light.

"Lachlan, what are you doing?" Daphne asked in a confused whisper. He pressed her hand to his cheek before he finally let go and stood.

"I..." He had no words, no way to tell her what lay in his heart at this moment.

"Forgive him, Miss Westfall," Cameron chuckled. "He seems to have swallowed his tongue."

"Aye, I have," he agreed with a smile and held out his arm to her. They entered the church together, the stained glass lighting up the pews with brilliant splashes of color.

The vicar, Mr. McKenzie, waited for them at the altar. Eliza and Cameron flanked them as the priest began his speech. Lachlan spoke his vows and stared at Daphne, smiling as they swore to love, honor and cherish each other until the day death parted them. The priest then pressed her right wrist against Lachlan's, and wound a plain white cloth around their hands. It was an old handfasting custom. Lachlan saw Daphne's puzzlement and fought off a chuckle. Then the priest spoke in Gaelic, and, in quiet whispers, Lachlan translated for her, "Two souls made one, two hearts made one. Let none tear asunder what the heavens have brought together."

Daphne's eyes widened as she looked up at him, but he saw only excitement with a hint of nervousness within her eyes, no fear.

"All right, lass?" he asked.

"Yes." As she spoke, a loose curl from her coiffure brushed her collarbone. He was arrested by the contrast of that lock against her pale skin, and the gleaming pearls that hung around her neck like frozen dewdrops along a delicate spider's web.

My lady in pearls.

"You may kiss your bride," Mr. McKenzie announced.

Lachlan leaned down, his free hand still curled in hers, their other hands bound fast, and kissed her. Tonight, he would see her in his bed, wearing nothing but those pearls, and he would make her smile, make her laugh, make her as happy as she was making him in that moment. When their lips broke apart, he heard her breathless sigh and reached up to brush her chin with his fingertips.

"You finally belong to me."

She caught his wrist and stroked his skin beneath the cuff of his shirtsleeve. "And you to me."

"Indeed." *I will not let the past destroy us.* The pain of William's death was finally muted, like a painting left in a sunny room, the colors bleached white, leaving barely a hint of what had once been so vivid. Daphne would paint new memories for him, ones of joy, not sorrow.

His throat tightened as the priest removed the hand bindings.

"I present Lord and Lady Huntley."

Cameron clapped loudly along with Eliza and Moira, who both wiped their eyes. For some glorious, ridiculous reason, Lachlan laughed, unable to contain the joy in his heart.

"I suppose you have a feast ready at home, Mother?"

Moira smiled despite her tears. "Of course. It's not every day my wee bairn takes a wife."

"Wee bairn?" Cameron laughed harder than Lachlan. "He's not been wee in over twenty years!"

"Mother, you mustn't embarrass me in front of my wife," he teased. "No man wishes to be thought of as wee on his wedding day."

Cameron laughed. "Indeed! Or Daphne will worry what else is wee on you tonight when you—*Oomph*!" Cameron doubled over as Eliza elbowed him hard in the chest.

Daphne giggled and Lachlan curled an arm around her waist.

"I promise, lass, there's nothing wee about me." He laughed again as she blushed scarlet.

The small wedding party exited the church and for the first time in two months, Lachlan embraced the warmth of the sun on his face. Daphne was his wife and tonight he would show her a world of pleasure. Perhaps Anthony had been right after all.

She will heal me. She's already begun to.

❧

MARRIED. I AM MARRIED.

Daphne couldn't stop smiling as she waited in Lachlan's bed chambers. It was close to midnight, but she wasn't tired. They'd spent the remainder of the day feasting and playing games in the drawing room with Cameron and Eliza. It had been the most fun she'd had in such a long time.

She plucked nervously now at the nightgown she'd changed into. The only thing she wore aside from it was her mother's pearls. Lachlan had stopped her in the corridor just before she'd left to change for bed. He caught her by the waist and leaned close to whisper, "Wear the pearls, and nothing else."

She couldn't very well wait in his chambers completely naked, but she assumed he would insist upon her removing her nightgown once he arrived.

The sound of footfalls outside the door made her tense. She curled her fingers into the fabric of her nightgown.

Lachlan entered. He carried a delicate decanter of wine

and a pair of glasses. He froze when he saw her standing there by his bed, barefoot, her hair unbound, wearing nothing but her nightclothes. He blinked and then gave his head a little shake.

"I thought you might wish for a drink." He gave the decanter a slight whirl and she nodded. A drink would help calm her nerves.

"Yes, that would be nice." She fidgeted for a moment before sitting down in the chair next to his desk. He poured two glasses and, after slipping one glass into her hand, drank his in two long gulps. He refilled his glass and brought it to his lips.

"Lachlan..." she began, noticing his hands shaking a little. Was he nervous? The thought was laughable. The worldly Scotsman, nervous on his wedding night?

"I..." He chuckled and set his glass down. "I am a wee bit..." He didn't finish, but his cheeks darkened to a ruddy shade beneath the candlelight.

"You're not the virgin, I am," she blurted out, and then covered her mouth with her hand, stifling a nervous laugh. Lachlan approached and played with the strands of her hair with his fingers, making her shiver with a secret thrill.

"I've not been with a lass that I cared about the way I do you." He brushed her long dark hair away from her neck. She reached up and touched the pearls at the same moment he did. Heat flared between them when their hands met.

"You care about me?" the words that escaped her were barely above a whisper.

His short nod was followed with a smile so faint she almost wondered if she'd imagined it.

Daphne held her breath a long moment before she replied, "I feel the same about you."

His look of boyish wonder as he cupped her face and

gazed into her eyes melted away every concern she'd had about marrying him.

"I doona deserve you, lass. But I swear on my bones that I will strive every day, with every breath, to care for you and make you happy." There was an almost violent flash of pain in his eyes. She threw her arms around his neck, clinging to him. She slipped off the chair and they tumbled onto the floor, Lachlan holding her in his lap as he leaned against the bed's frame.

Daphne breathed in his comforting, enticing masculine scent and pressed her lips to his neck. His hands tightened around her waist as he held her very still. She examined his face, the hard jaw with a hint of stubble, his blue eyes now as dark and endless as the surface of a lake.

She trailed her fingertips down his nose to his lips, memorizing every curve, every faint line, even the barest hint of freckles on the bridge of his nose, which she hadn't noticed before. He was beautiful physically, but there was something else, a nobility in his face that seem to come from within. It had nothing to do with bloodlines or titles, but a nobility of the soul. She realized she trusted him more than she had ever trusted anyone except her mother. Her father's crimes had cost her much, including her trust in others, but now, for the first time, she felt like she could trust another person. She could trust in Lachlan.

I want to give him everything, all that I am.

"Are you ready to go to bed?" she asked, stroking his lips. He moved one hand up and down her back, the way a man would calm an untamed horse.

"Aye. Are you?" he asked. Worry marred his face until she nodded.

She slid off his lap and they stood, smiling hesitantly, both embarrassed.

"Why don't I take off my shirt?" He stepped back and

reached over his head to pull off the white garment. Once exposed to view, his bare chest made her mouth run dry. He tossed the shirt away and lifted one of her hands to his chest, placing her palm over his heart.

"I am yours, lass, look your fill. *Touch.*" He stroked the back of her hand. "As you will."

Daphne explored him, marveling at the muscled plains of his abdomen and the corded steel of his arms, awed that something so beautiful could be hers. Then he unfastened his trousers and removed his shoes. She stepped back with wide eyes when she saw his fully bared body. He was unashamed and waved her closer with a coaxing hand. He stepped back and leaned on the edge of the bed, inviting her near.

"I doona bite," he chuckled when she drew close enough. She placed one hand on the top of his hard thigh, a secret delight surging through her when his muscles leapt beneath her fingers.

"Now for you." He reached for the front of her nightgown, unfastened the buttons at her breasts and then lifted the gown over her head.

When she stood naked before him, she stiffened, her nipples pebbling in the cool air. He parted his knees and gently pulled her to stand between his thighs so he could touch her. He cupped one breast, and his rough, calloused palms sent delightful tingles through her. She clenched her thighs as wetness grew between them.

Lachlan plucked one nipple, the gentle tug making her hiss out a soft moan. She arched her back, clutching his shoulders as she offered him her other breast. He bent his head and fastened his mouth to it, kissing, sucking, nibbling until she couldn't stop from trembling. Everything he did was thrilling, even frightening, but exquisitely wonderful. She reached for his erect shaft, needing to touch him as intimately as he was touching her, but he caught her wrist.

"There will be plenty of time for that, lass, but not yet. A man needs to pleasure his woman thoroughly before he sees to himself." He slid his hands down to her bottom and lifted her onto his lap. His shaft slid between her wet folds and she whimpered as a hard edge of need rolled through her. She needed him to do something to her, to ease the hunger she barely understood.

"Lachlan, please, I want you to—"

"Shhh..." He kissed her hungrily, their lips melding as he clenched her buttocks and rocked her against him in his lap. She arched, her knees sliding on the bedding on either side of his slender hips. Daphne was desperate to feel him inside her, even though she was afraid he wouldn't fit, that he was far too big, but her hunger was stronger than her concerns. They broke the kiss and she implored him with begging eyes to give her what she needed, what they both did.

"Aye. You'll be the death of me, wife." He fell back on the bed with her before he rolled them over so that she lay beneath him. Her knees gripped his hips, trying to close even though his body lay between them. Blood surged from her fingertips to her toes.

He lowered his mouth to hers, and his kiss burned like morning light through the darkness of her weary soul and she surrendered everything to him. The unexpected pinch she felt as he slid inside her faded beneath the fire of his kiss. He spoke to her between kisses as he withdrew and thrust back inside her. She recognized the words, the Gaelic from the wedding ceremony.

"Two souls made one, two hearts made one. Let none tear asunder what the heavens have brought together." She closed her eyes as the tension building inside her broke in a sudden crest. The pleasure was as pure as it was explosive. Daphne gasped in sweet agony. She clung to him, her inner walls fluttering around him and she pressed frantic kisses along his cheek, lips and chin as he thrust twice more and collapsed on top of her, his weight heavy but welcome.

Lachlan kissed the shell of her ear, smiling as he lifted his head to gaze down at her. A deep peace settled inside her, as if she stood in a meadow at dawn, with the birds beginning to chatter softly, sunlight beginning to bathe the ground, and a breeze rustling the grass.

There was something about a *beginning*. It seemed to fill one's soul with hope, with *love*. What she and Lachlan had shared this night was a new dawn, a beginning all their own.

Lachlan brushed stray wisps of hair back from her face and swallowed hard. "How do you feel?" he asked.

Daphne smiled, feeling like her whole body could float away. "As though you gave me wings to fly."

With a chuckle and a glint of mischief in his eyes, he nuzzled her cheek. "I've not even showed you the best parts."

"Oh?" She couldn't possibly imagine that what they had just done could get any better.

"Aye, there's a few hours yet before we should sleep. And I know just how we can pass the time." He kissed her, and she was swept away by his embrace, his touch and his passion. Lachlan had given her the one thing she longed for above all else. Happiness. She would cling to it as long as she could.

9

"You're in love with her."

Lachlan tensed. He and Cameron leaned against the short wall of the terrace. Before them, in the field between the gardens, Daphne and Eliza played with a sheepdog that belonged to one of the tenant farmers who had come to speak with Lachlan's groundskeeper.

"No, I like her. She's a bonnie lass and—"

"You can lie to yourself, old friend, but never to me." Cameron's teasing tone softened, "I know you've convinced yourself you don't deserve love, not after losing William, but you're wrong. You deserve her. You deserve joy in your life. It's what he would have wanted for you."

Cameron touched Lachlan's shoulder. The truth of his friend's words seemed to reverberate through his body with the sound and clarity of the bells hanging in the tower of the Kirk of Huntley.

He *loved* Daphne.

He should've known the first time he spoke with her that she would leave a burning imprint upon his heart and soul.

Lachlan was finally seeing things clearly. It mattered that her father had driven William to his death, but she was not her father. His sins were not hers, and would never be hers. She was a victim, just like William, yet she hadn't surrendered, hadn't given up, even when she had reached the end of her rope. She'd agreed to marry a stranger, and done her best to fit in here. She had even fallen in love with him. Even now, without knowing it, she had changed him, dragged him kicking and screaming from the hollow hole in his heart and forced him back into the light of the living, How could he not love her?

Daphne tossed a red ball and the sheepdog scampered across the lawn, stumbling to a stop as he nearly tripped over his prey, then clutched it in his mouth and returned it to her. He shook his black and white coat and pawed the ground before dropping the ball, his tail wagging so hard that his whole body shook. Even at this distance, Lachlan could see the joy on Daphne's face.

"There it is again," Cameron said. "That love-struck look you made fun of me for when I first told you I planned to marry Eliza."

Lachlan couldn't resist a smile. "I suppose I am owed this teasing, aren't I?"

"Indeed, you are, and more." Cameron chuckled. "I think it's time Eliza and I went home. You need a proper honeymoon with your bride, and should not spend it entertaining guests."

Lachlan grinned. "As much as I like you, I would prefer to return her to bed and not leave for days except to eat."

Cameron slapped Lachlan's shoulder. "Let me collect my wife. We should arrive home in time for dinner."

Lachlan shook hands once more with his friend. As he watched Cameron walk away, he realized he'd neglected their friendship for too long. William's death had robbed him of so much: his joy, his friends. Marrying Daphne was already bringing his life back into focus. He wouldn't let the things that truly mattered escape him again.

Lachlan remained on the terrace, watching Daphne chase the dog, who now barked excitedly and dodged her in a game as old as time. The heartache in his chest was nearly gone, something he never thought possible.

"My lord?"

Lachlan turned away from the terrace. His groundskeeper stood there before him, hat in hand.

"Yes?"

"The farmers said the black fallow deer herds are in need of thinning. I thought we might give them permission to go shooting on our lands, if you approve."

"Of course. You'll see to it they get the meat they need?"

His groundskeeper nodded, then laughed. Lachlan followed his gaze back to the field. Daphne held the dog's front paws, making him stand on hind legs. The furry beast was licking her face enthusiastically.

"Oh, I'll see to it. You got a bonnie bride to tend to quickly, or else you might be replaced in her affections." The groundskeeper chuckled as he walked away.

Lachlan leaned against the stone terrace railing and watched his bride. Her hair blew loose in the breeze, her face flushed. She waved at him and he waved back, a boyish giddiness growing inside him. After so much darkness, so much pain, he had a moment of pure contentment.

Daphne left the dog and walked up to the steps.

"It's a wonderful day. Come and walk with me." She held out her hand.

He descended the stairs and took it, loving how their fingers intertwined, and headed toward the gardens. Once there, he tugged her against his body, delighting in her gasp and sigh as he covered her mouth with his. Daphne gave freely of herself and he whispered soft words of encouragement against her skin when she clung to him. The velvet warmth of her kisses cocooned him inside a private heaven that he never wished to leave.

He wasn't sure how much time passed before they broke apart. That single kiss had seemed endless. He never knew that simply kissing a woman could fill him with such pleasure.

Lachlan grasped her hands and grinned. "Let's go inside and continue this."

She giggled. "That sounds like a wonderful idea."

As they walked back to the house, Lachlan had to stop himself from whistling. In the distance, he heard the crack of gunfire.

"What's that?" Daphne asked, looking over the fields beyond the castle.

"The farmers are hunting deer. The herds need thinning. I have quite a few on Huntley lands, and I let the tenants hunt during the winter to keep the poor beasts from starving. The extra meat will be a welcome for the tenant farmers come wintertime."

"Can I meet the tenants?" she asked. "I would like to know as much as possible about your life here."

"*Our* life," he corrected.

"Our life," she echoed with a blush.

"I can take you to meet them tomorrow." Lachlan paused as he reached the door and stole one more kiss before he gestured for her to precede him.

"Lachlan?" His mother's voice stopped him in his tracks.

Moira stood in the hallway, her face pale. She clutched a piece of paper. She stood only a few feet from his study, or rather, William's study. Moira's eyes darted to Daphne, a mixture of horror and pain so stark it made him suck in a breath.

She knew.

"Moira, are you all right?" Daphne let go of Lachlan's arm and started toward her. Moira retreated a step as though Daphne would attack her.

"I need to speak with you, *alone*." Moira told him, refusing to look at Daphne.

"Lachlan, should I...?" Daphne began.

"Go upstairs to my chambers and wait from me." He moved toward his wife.

"But—"

"Go." He pushed her gently toward the stairs.

Once he was sure Daphne had reached the upper floor, he escorted his mother into William's study and closed the door.

"You *hid* this from me." His mother shoved the paper at his chest and he caught the slightly crumpled letter. "I found it locked in his desk drawer. You *knew*, didn't you? William never locked those drawers, but *you* did." Moira's eyes were rimmed with red as she looked at him, then she collapsed into a chair in front of William's desk, her head bowed.

"I couldn't let you know the truth." He set the letter down on the escritoire, his throat suddenly tight. Why hadn't he burned the letter? He should have, but he'd foolishly been unable to let go of it. They were William's last words and he couldn't let go.

His mother lifted her head. "He said he was involved in something with Sir Richard Westfall. That's Daphne's father, isn't it?" It was less a question than an accusation.

"Yes." He wanted to lie to her, but he couldn't.

"You knew before you married her, didn't you?" Moira sniffed. Tears trickled down her cheeks. His mother's agony cut through him hard enough that he could feel his heart bleeding.

"Aye. I knew."

"But ...how could you? The daughter of the man who-- Why? Did you think to find some justice in it or did you have other designs for her? What were you thinking?" her words crumbled into a breathless inhalation as she fought off a sob.

"I married her to hurt her, to hurt *him*. I didn't love her, mother. It was a marriage arranged from spite and vengeance. I wanted to make her miserable. It was my only way to hurt him, through her." A great weariness settled on him.

"What?" Moira's voice cracked. "You brought her here for that? Lachlan, I want her gone, I can't have her here, not when..." she choked on a sob and wiped her eyes. "She's a sweet girl and she doesn't deserve to suffer your vengeance. She's not her father, can't you see? Living with a man who despises her isn't fair to her, not when she's innocent of her father's crimes. You must send her back to London. Annul the marriage."

"It's too late for that," he whispered.

His mother stared at him, horror filling her face. "Then you must live apart."

Lachlan was silent for a long moment. "No. I can't send her away. Because... I love her. I love her *wildly*, Mother. I don't care about her father, not anymore. I want to look forward, not dwell in the past. She's the only thing that matters to me now. William would not have wanted me to forsake my love if he knew how happy I could be."

Moira rose from the chair, her blue eyes dull and her lips trembling.

"You should have told me." For a long moment they stared at each other, a chasm growing between them, one that he feared he could not repair. Then she turned her back on him and left.

For a long while he didn't move. He stood behind

William's desk, thinking back to the day he'd ridden up to the house and saw his brother in the window, heard the shot that rang out across the grounds, and the awful silence that followed. His heart had frozen in that instant as he had tried to reach his brother. Too late. Always, too late.

"I'm sorry, brother," he whispered to the silent room. He could almost feel William there, as though he paused on the other side of an invisible veil. The hairs on the back of his neck rose and he closed his eyes, speaking again. "I *love* her. I can't cling to both love and hate. She fills my heart, so there's no room left for anger and pain and hatred."

He thought for a brief moment that a hand touched his shoulder. An infinitesimal pressure, one of reassurance and comfort. He reached up and placed his hand where he felt the slight weight.

"There is nothing to forgive," the words came in William's voice.

His mother would need time to heal, to understand. Right now, he needed to speak to Daphne. She deserved to know the truth. But first he had to prove his love for her. Only then could he confess the truth behind his original intentions in marrying her.

As he exited the study, he heard something roll along the wooden floor. He glanced down and saw two dozen white beads that had scattered when his foot brushed them. He knelt and picked one up. They were pearls. Not his mother's, because she hadn't worn any.

With a gasp, he frantically tried to retrieve the pearls, clutching them in his palm. Blood roared in his ears as he reached into the nooks and crannies of the hall, desperate to reclaim every precious orb. But Daphne had gone upstairs, so how...?

"May I help you, my lord?" The young maid, Mary, knelt

beside him, cupping her hands to receive what he'd collected so far.

"Take these and put them somewhere safe. We must find every one," he said. His voice began to fill with panic, trying not to think about the implications of this moment.

The maid tucked the pearls into her apron pocket. "My lord, the countess is gone."

His stomach grew heavy as his fear began to materialize, but still he refused to believe it. "Gone?"

"She was crying, and I feared you didn't know. She called for a coach and left."

There was no more denial left in him. Daphne must have listened at the door. He stared at the floor where the pearls had fallen. She always touched them when she was anxious. She must have ripped them from her neck before she fled, when she heard the awful truth behind their marriage.

"How long ago did she leave?"

"Half an hour?" Mary guessed.

"What? Why did no one summon me?" He stumbled to his feet.

The maid stepped back but was brave enough to answer, "She was most upset when you were in the study and begged the staff who saw her not to say a word. But when I saw you come out, I knew someone had to tell you." Her gaze shot to the open door behind him and he understood. No one bothered him when he was inside his study. They believed he went in there to seek peace, to feel close to William, and it was true.

"I'll take care of the pearls, my lord," Mary promised, one hand touching the pocket of her apron.

"Thank you." Lachlan sprinted down the corridor and called for the nearest footman to have a horse saddled. He donned a coat and gloves as he rushed down the steps to the drive. He studied the road leading away from Huntley Castle but saw no sign of the coach carrying Daphne away from him.

Lachlan nodded at the groom who brought him his fastest gelding and mounted. He prayed he would not be too late to reach the other half of his heart before it, too, was lost forever.

10

Daphne could barely breathe.

She lay curled up in the coach, a fisted hand pressed against her mouth to mute the sound of her sobs. Why had she gone back downstairs? She had hoped to render aid to Moira in some way, who had clearly been distressed, but then the words she'd overheard had stopped her cold and eventually broken her soul.

Until that moment, she'd survived everything. Her father's scandal, the loss of her former life, her home and friends, but none of it hurt quite like losing her heart. Everything had been a lie. Every kiss, every look, every vow to love and cherish each other. All she'd had to hear was that her marriage to him was a lie and she'd fled the house.

I was nothing more than a part of Lachlan's vengeance.

She reached for her neck. The skin was bare, yet it stung where she'd grabbed her mother's pearls and ripped them off in panic as her world fell apart.

She'd had recurring dreams of drowning in her youth, of being pulled down into an endless darkness, her mouth and lungs filling with water. Lachlan's words were worse than those nightmares. They weren't just pulling her down, they were burying her so far below the surface that she would never survive.

"It was a marriage of spite and revenge."

Tears leaked from her eyes as she recalled the heat of his kiss, the whispered words of affection in her ear, and their bodies pressed close.

All lies. He had treated her well. So, when had he planned to spring his trap? She didn't want to stay and find out what his form of revenge would be.

She tried to breathe again, but air got trapped between her mouth and her lungs, unable to flow. The coach rocked suddenly and a voice outside shouted, "Halt!"

Lachlan's commanding tone was all too clear. It jolted Daphne's heart back into rhythm. The carriage bumped to a sudden stop.

"My lord?" the driver called out.

Daphne heard steps on the left side of the coach. She jerked open the door on the right and tumbled into the road. They had reached the forest a mile from the castle. Her attention swept the tall, dark woods, the thick trunks and the cover of the head pine trees. There was nowhere to run, but she couldn't stay here.

"Daphne?" Lachlan's voice sounded hoarse and panicked.

She wiped tears from her face and ran past the horses and the stunned coach driver. She heard a curse and the rush of boots on the dirt road behind her. A hand caught her arm, dragging her to a halt. The pull sent her spinning back around to face him. He caught her in his arms and for an awful instant her body wanted to surrender, to burrow into him and believe the lies he'd told her, if only for a little while. She regained control and shoved at his chest.

"Let go of me, you monster!"

"Daphne, please listen," Lachlan begged, holding her tight despite her struggles.

She kicked his shin. He cursed, bent to grasp his leg and let go. Stunned by her sudden freedom, she didn't immediately turn to leave. What would be the point? She could not outrun him.

Lachlan straightened, letting go of his shin as he panted and stared at her. "Please, let me explain."

"Why should I?" The words cut her, but she kept her head high. Her father may have committed terrible crimes, but she was also the granddaughter of a duke and a lady in her own right. What pride she had left wouldn't allow her to be pathetic, not even when her heart was bleeding.

"I know what you heard." Lachlan's face reddened. "My motives the night we met were inexcusable. Monstrous, yes. My heart was blackened with grief and you came into my life offering what I thought I needed." He swallowed hard, then his words dropped to a whisper as he gazed at her like a drowning man would stare at a rope tossed to him from shore. "And I was right. You *were* what I needed... I just didn't know the reasons why."

Daphne wasn't sure she understood what he was saying.

"I didn't need revenge. I needed...*love*." The last word was spoken so softly she thought perhaps she might have dreamt it. He reached for her and she didn't draw away, even though she knew she should. With gentle fingers, he brushed away the tears on her cheeks.

"You don't love me," she said, her voice hitching. "You don't intend to hurt people you love."

The smile he gave was bittersweet. "I agree. But every time I tried to hurt you, to revenge William's death, I stopped. I couldn't go through with it. Did you not hear what I told my mother?"

"That you married me out of spite and vengeance? What

happens when you are in one of your black moods? When you miss William and all you see in my eyes is the daughter of the man responsible? Will you still love me then?"

"You are not your father. I see that now." He raked a hand through his hair. "You didn't hear the rest. You didn't hear me say that I love you. I love you madly. I love you with a wildness that frightens me."

He took a step closer to her, his blue eyes stark with desperation. She didn't step away, but her heart raced. She had to master her reactions as he held out a hand to her. Loneliness and confusion battled with hope and longing until the crescendo of emotions became too overwhelming to be kept inside. She sniffed as her nose and eyes began to burn.

"Will you say something, lass? Anything?" he begged.

"How do I know you mean what you say? Any of it?"

Lachlan looked away, then locked eyes with her again. His throat worked as he tugged at his cravat. "I don't know a way to prove it to you. I'm a man full of stubborn, foolish pride, but..." He took her hand and knelt down on one knee. The memory of the last time he'd done this came flooding back. The tears which followed burned her cheeks, but she didn't move to wipe them away, or dare to breathe.

He paused, his blue eyes misty. "I found your pearls. They'd spilled across the floor and I picked them up, every single one and..." He shook his head, as though unsure of what to say, then, "I was never supposed to be an earl. That was William. But he's gone, and I am here, making a bloody mess of everything I hold dear. I understand why the pearls are so important to you. You, you are *my* string of pearls, Daphne. The thing I reach for when I'm full of joy or when I'm frightened of the world around me. You are the most precious thing to me. You are my hope."

He stroked his thumbs over her cheeks, his gaze impossibly soft. "In my eyes, you are the most exquisite gift a man could be given. I'm afraid to let you go, to have you scatter and vanish like a broken strand of pearls." He bowed his head. "But if you must leave, I love you too much to force you to stay." Lachlan drew in a deep breath, pressing her hand to his cheek.

"You'd really let me go?" she asked.

"Yes, but you'd take my heart with you, lass." He choked on the last few words. And, in that moment, she saw him in a way she hadn't before. She saw Lachlan's heart beneath the tall muscled form that remained on bended knee before her. His heart was in his eyes and the pain of his past, so vividly exposed, that she hurt with him. There was no menace, no anger or hatred there, only love and the fear of losing it. But it all brought one question to mind, one she still didn't know the answer to.

"*Why* do you love me?"

He answered without hesitation, "Because of who you are. Not as the daughter of a wretched man, but as a woman who cares about strangers and fights for her life and refuses to surrender to fate. A woman who smiles and dances and finds joy even after enduring so much sorrow. You love with all your heart and make me want to be the best version of myself. I can't breathe when I think of you hurting, lass. You've become a part of me, and I hope that there's a little bit of me inside you too. I cannot imagine my life without you." He pressed his lips to her hand. "I made a vow in the church to you. Two souls made one, two hearts made one. The heavens brought us together and only you can break us apart."

Daphne stared down at him, too afraid to hope that all he said was true.

"Lachlan, even if I believe you, it won't erase the fact that my father caused your brother's death. Your mother will never forgive me."

He was on his feet, tugging her into his arms, embracing

her so tight that she had to shove at him to get room to breathe.

"All that matters, is that you are my wife, my love. What your father did was a true dishonor, but William was his own man. He took his own life by his own choice. I didn't want to face that truth, but I have to. Tragedy brought you to me, but I promise to let only hope bind us from now on."

She pressed her cheek to his chest, her heart still heavy with concern. "What about Moira?"

"She likes you. She wanted you gone to protect you from me and my thirst for vengeance. But my only plan is to love you. Madly, wildly, deeply." He leaned back so he could cup her face.

"Lachlan," she breathed, trembling, wanting to believe him, to trust him.

He brushed a thumb over her lips so intently that he seemed to be imprinting their shape upon his memory. "Aye?"

"You cannot lie to me, ever again. I need...I *deserve* a husband who loves me enough to give me honesty. If you won't be that man, then I have to leave." She was amazed at the strength in her voice. She meant every word. She would protect herself no matter the consequences.

Lachlan nodded. "Aye, you're right. And you have my word. I am your man, lass. Always." The word was breathed so softy it sounded like a prayer.

By the forest's edge, a deer wandered out and watched their reunion with mild interest.

"Then take me home." Home to Huntley. Home with him.

Please let him be a man of his word. Please let him love me.

Lachlan laughed with such joy and relief that he swung her around in the air before he set her back down.

"Ach, lass," he murmured, kissing her. "You'll be the death of me if I lose you."

"Then don't lose me." She bit her lip but finally smiled after a moment. She was so afraid to hope they could be happy—

Crack!

The report of a rifle exploded around them and the deer bolted across the road. Lachlan grunted and stumbled, still holding her in his arms, but she saw pain streak across his features before he dropped his arms and crumpled to the ground.

Blood suddenly covered her face and his.

"Lachlan!" She screamed, falling to her knees by his side.

"My lord!" The driver leapt from the coach and dashed over to Lachlan.

"He's bleeding!" Daphne touched Lachlan's head. Blood poured from a deep cut along one of his temples.

"He's been shot."

"What?" Daphne frantically ripped at the hem of her dress, freeing a bit of fabric. She pressed it to the wound, staunching it. Terror pounded inside her.

Shot. Blood. Death. The three words cut through her over and over as she pressed the cloth tight to Lachlan's head.

"Seamus! You shot his lordship!" Both the driver and Daphne looked in the direction of sounds coming from the nearby underbrush. An old man and a young boy emerged from the foliage. The young boy carried a rifle. The old man shook the young boy by the shoulders and tore the rifle from his hands.

Seamus's face turned ashen as he stared at Daphne and the coach driver clutching Lachlan's body, blood coating their hands and the road.

"I dinnae mean to!" The lad's bottom lip quivered.

"Help me get him into the coach," she told the driver. She turned to the farmer and boy. "Do you have horses?"

"Aye."

"Fetch the nearest doctor. Send him to the castle."

The old man struck the boy's backside. "You heard her ladyship!"

Seamus sprinted back into the underbrush. The farmer helped Daphne and the driver lift Lachlan into the coach. The farmer stayed inside with Daphne, who kept the blood-soaked bit of cloth pressed tight to Lachlan's temple.

The ride back to the castle seemed to last forever. Daphne panted softly as she focused on Lachlan. His eyes opened halfway, as if he were dreaming and not losing a perilous amount of blood.

"My pearl," Lachlan said drowsily and raised one hand to brush her cheek.

She clasped his hand in hers. "I'm here." His eyes closed but his breathing remained steady. When they reached Huntley Castle, Daphne ordered the farmer and driver to carry Lachlan to the drawing room.

Moira rushed down the steps. "Lachlan!"

"He was grazed by a bullet." Daphne caught Moira's arm. "Have the footmen bring hot water and fresh towels."

Moira whirled and rushed into the house, calling for footmen. Daphne led the driver and the farmer into the drawing room, where they placed him on a chaise lounge.

She continued to keep the cloth firmly pressed to his wound the entire time.

"What else can I do, my lady?" the farmer asked.

"Watch for the doctor."

She wiped the blood on the side of Lachlan's head, wincing.

"What happened?" Moira's voice broke as she rushed into the room, two footmen following, their arms full of supplies.

"Hold this." She took Moira's hand and pressed it against the cloth to keep pressure on Lachlan's wound. Then she stood and took one of the cloths from a footman. She offered him a whisper of thanks before she dipped the cloth in the bowl of hot water. She returned to Lachlan and pressed a new, clean cloth to his temple.

"Daphne, what happened?" Moira demanded again.

"One of the tenant farmer's children was hunting and the bullet grazed Lachlan's head. If it's only a surface wound, he will be all right. Head wounds bleed more than others."

Moira's eyes were pinned to her son's pale face. "How do you know?"

"My father had friends who served in the military and shared rather vivid memories from the wars. One of them mentioned that a head wound such as this bled a lot, but wasn't fatal as long as the injured person was seen by a physician right away.

There was a commotion outside the drawing room and the boy from the forest appeared. Behind him came a gentleman in a black waistcoat and trousers. He carried a black medicine bag as he rushed to Lachlan's side.

Moira and Daphne gave the doctor space to examine Lachlan's head wound. Moira slipped a hand in hers and they clung to each other, holding their breaths while the doctor tended to Lachlan. He spent several minutes closing the wound with stiches and then cleansed it. When he finished, he faced them with a relieved smile.

"His Lordship should be fine. He'll need his bandages changed daily until the wound fully heals. No riding, bending over, or anything else that requires physical exertion until the stiches have been removed."

Daphne glanced at Moira and then she turned back to the doctor. "I believe we can manage that."

"What can we do for him now?"

"For now, you must let him rest. I will leave you some further instructions before I go."

"Thank you." Moira wiped away a tear before she shooed the footmen away.

"I'll be back with some hot tea," Moira said before she, too, slipped out of the room.

After Daphne thanked the doctor and saw him out, she returned to Lachlan's side and set a chair next to the chaise, thankful she could just sit beside him. She curled her fingers around his hand. He had protected her when she was desperate for help. Now she would protect him.

A few minutes later, Moira returned with tea and poured them both a cup.

"Is he doing better?" she asked.

Daphne had been paying close attention to Lachlan's breathing. It had deepened rather than become shallow. That was a good sign.

"Yes. I think so."

Moira swallowed hard and looked at Daphne. "I pray you are right. I cannot lose him, not like I did William."

Daphne placed a hand over Moira's wrist, squeezing it gently. "You won't lose him."

"You are so sure... How?"

Daphne smiled sadly. "Because Lachlan is a fighter. He won't let go of life, not without a struggle. It's one of the reasons I love him."

"You love him?" Moira's eyes softened with sorrow. "But you must know why he brought you here."

"I overheard you talking in the study. It's why I left. What I didn't hear was that his feelings had changed."

"He said he loved you. I know my son. He spoke the truth when he said he loved you. I didn't want to believe, but it was in his eyes, in his voice." Moira stroked Lachlan's cheek and he groaned.

"If he can love you, then I believe I can too," Moira said. "I already was fond of you, my dear. I couldn't have chosen a better woman for him. Fortunately, I didn't need to."

Daphne's throat constricted as she focused on Lachlan, afraid she might burst into tears if she looked at Moira right now. It was all she ever wanted, to be accepted and loved.

I'm so afraid it won't last, that this dream will prove false.

11

Lachlan woke, his mouth dry and his head throbbing. A soft weight rested on his ribs. He moved and felt a feminine body slumped over his chest. He blinked, clearing his vision, and saw Daphne sitting beside him on a chair in the drawing room.

What had happened?

The last thing he remembered was standing on the side of the road, holding her in his arms, after she agreed to return home. He reached for his temple and touched bandages. The drawing room door opened a crack and his mother peered inside. She looked between him and Daphne.

He carefully slipped off of the chaise, then eased Daphne back in her chair. He touched his head again gingerly, fighting off a wave of dizziness.

"You need to stay down," his mother admonished, trying to force him back to the chaise.

"I will, in a moment. I wish to speak with you outside first." He pointed to the hall. They both exited the room and he leaned against the corridor wall to preserve his strength while his head pounded.

"Lachlan, you scared me." His mother embraced him with a gentle, careful hug, reminding him of when he was a wee lad and he'd come to her afraid of shadows. She'd held him just like this and whispered the words only mothers knew that could put a child's fears to rest.

"I'm all right, Mother." He kissed her forehead and then gently lifted her arms away so she would step back. He needed to see her face and he couldn't do that while she hugged him.

"I was so afraid," Moira's voice trembled. "I couldn't lose you too."

"You didn't. I'm right here." He looked back through the doorway, where he could still see Daphne's blood covered, sleeping form.

"She's a sweet, brave lass and I want her to stay," Moira said. "She loves you, despite the terrible reason you brought her here."

"I love her more than I ever thought I could love a woman. I thought, at first, fate was being cruel by letting me fall in love with the daughter of the man who drove William to his death, but she's suffered too. Greatly. And when I'm with her, my heart doesn't feel so broken."

Moira hugged him again. "Maybe we can finally heal."

"Aye."

"My lord?"

Lachlan turned. Mary stood behind them. She held a small rosewood box on her palm. "I collected each pearl. What should I do with them?"

Lachlan glanced at his mother. "I have an idea. Assuming you don't mind, Mother." He winked when she raised her brows.

"What are you up to, Lachlan?" she asked.

"Something wonderful."

A WEEK LATER, DAPHNE SAT CURLED IN A LIBRARY CHAIR, reading by the fire. Beside her, in his own chair, Lachlan pretended to read. His head wound was nearly healed after she'd spent every day looking after him. This was the first day in which he'd insisted she take a few hours to do something she enjoyed and not fuss over him. When she'd suggested reading in the library, he'd agreed. Yet from the moment they'd sat down with their books, his focus remained on her. Every so often, she looked up and he hastily returned his attention to his book.

"You're watching me," she said. "Why?"

He smiled, set his book aside, and waved her over. She put her own book down, crawled onto his lap, and wrapped her arms around his neck.

"I've been waiting for the right time to give you this." He reached into his trouser pocket and pulled out a small, velvet pouch. He offered it on his palm. She took it, loosened the drawstrings, opened the velvet. She paused and looked at Lachlan in puzzlement before she tilted the bag upside down. Pearls tumbled into her hand. This necklace held two strands of pearls.

"My pearls... But... they can't be. Mother's necklace had only a single strand of pearls."

"The others are a gift from my mother. She would have given them to you at some point."

"But, I cannot take hers, not when..."

"Hush, lass. She wanted you to have them. To let you know that you're as dear to her as you are to me."

Daphne peered closely at the double-strand necklace, her lips trembling.

She pressed the back of her fingers against her mouth. "I

thought I'd lost them forever when I left that day. I'd thought I'd lost you too," she admitted.

"I'm not that easy to be rid of, you know." His tone was teasing and mischief lit his eyes.

"I know. You almost died and..." she choked, the terror of that day still fresh in her mind. She could have lost him forever.

"But I didn't, now dry those eyes. I don't ever want to see you crying on my account." He wiped at a tear that trailed down her face.

She sniffled and raised the necklace to her cheek, brushing the smooth round orbs against her skin before she kissed them.

A piece of her past had been restored through Lachlan's thoughtfulness. Her heart had shattered violently from Lachlan's betrayal and she'd run fast and far from the dream world Lachlan had let her glimpse. When she'd broken the strand and the pearls had scattered across the floor, she hadn't stopped to retrieve them. She'd tried hard to forget the pearls over the last few days, not knowing what had happened when they'd fallen. They'd represented the life she'd had before her mother died, and she'd had to face the truth. That part of her life was over, had been over for years. She was living her new life, with man she loved with all of her heart. Yet he'd given her back this last bit of her mother and Moira had given her a set of pearls too. The unity of those two strands together was beautiful not because the pearls were lovely but because of what they represented. Time was healing old wounds. Willian's death and her father's imprisonment were the past. She and Lachlan were the future.

Lachlan took the pearls from her and fastened the clasp around her neck. Their gentle weight against her collarbones was comforting.

"I love you lass, never doubt it." Lachlan's winter-blue eyes held no frost, only the heat of a winter fire.

She brushed her fingers through his hair, careful not to touch his barely healed wound. "I love you too."

"Prove it," he said.

She brushed her nose against his. "You're quite commanding, aren't you?"

"Only when I expect to be kissed." He wrapped his arms around her waist and she laughed, but her heart was so full that she could scarcely breathe. She very slowly leaned her head into his, biting her lip as she paused an inch from his mouth.

"Do you know what I keep thinking about?" she asked.

"What?" His eyes fixed on her mouth.

"About our wedding, and the moment we entered the church together."

Lachlan's eyes met hers and held. "That is a day I will never forget. I could breathe again when I took you in my arms and pledged myself to you. You gave me my life back." He brushed a finger over the pearls. "My lady in pearls."

"You did the same for me." She closed the last inch between them. Their lips met and time froze, like an errant beam of sunlight that strikes a chandelier's crystal and fractures into a rainbow that illuminates the world around it.

We are two broken hearts made whole, two lost souls made one.

Wait! This isn't the end...I know you were panicking there for a minute right?
Well don't worry! The best way to know when a new book is released is to do one or all of the following:

Join my Newsletter:

http://laurensmithbooks.com/free-books-and-newsletter/

Follow Me on BookBub:
https://www.bookbub.com/authors/lauren-smith

Join my Facebook VIP Reader Group called Lauren Smith's League:
https://www.facebook.com/groups/400377546765661/

Want three free books?
You'll get *Wicked Designs* (a historical romance), *Legally Charming* (a contemporary romance) and *The Bite of Winter* (a paranormal romance). Fill out the form at the bottom of this link and you'll get an email from me with details to collect your free read!

Claim your free books now at:
http://laurensmithbooks.com/free-books-and-newsletter/,
follow me on twitter at @LSmithAuthor, or
like my Facebook page at
https://www.facebook.com/LaurenDianaSmith.
Join my PRIVATE Facebook VIP Reader group at:
https://www.facebook.com/groups/400377546765661/

I share upcoming book news, snippets and cover reveals plus PRIZES!

Reviews help other readers find books. I appreciate all reviews, whether positive or negative. If one of my books spoke to you, please share!

YOU'VE JUST READ BEWITCHING THE EARL. IF YOU like what you've read, feel free to explore another delicious and romantic series: Sins and Scandals!

Feel free to fall in love with Leo, the british Earl and the half gypsy woman from his childhood, Ivy as they rekindle their romance! Turn the page to read the first 3 chapters of *An Earl By Any Other Name*! Come on, you know you want to turn that page...

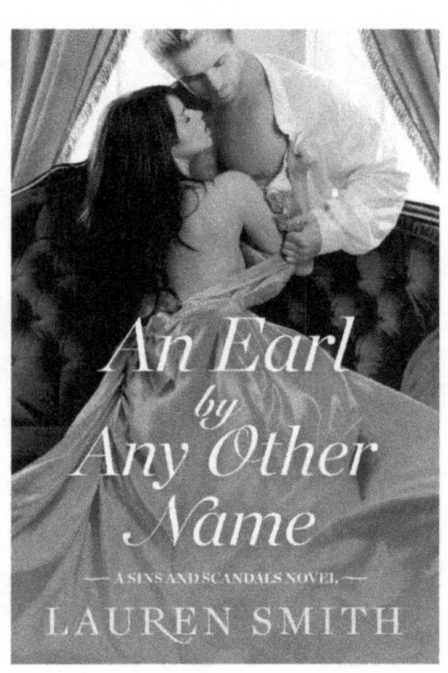

AN EARL BY ANY OTHER NAME

CHAPTER 1

England, October 1911

"You know what they say about the old boy..." Lord Caruthers murmured as Leopold Graham stepped into the main reading room of Brooks's Club on St. James's Street. The words stopped Leo cold.

"No...what do they say?" another man whispered, his face half hidden behind a newspaper. The two men were sitting close to a fireplace beside the door. They were both older, with graying hair and extended waistlines that showed their well-off lifestyles. Leo scowled at them, but deep inside he was afraid of their whispers.

"Kept an Italian opera singer in a cozy little love nest in Mayfair. Can you believe it?" Caruthers chuckled. "Damned if I'm not jealous of old Hampton for carrying on like that with a wife and son at home. Quite a bold move to bring down scandal like that so publically."

"Wait..." The other man gasped, his paper rattling in his hands with excitement as he leaned closer to Caruthers. "The old fellow who died in his mistress's bed? I heard about that!" The older gentlemen were leaning close to each other, gossiping like a pair of old ladies, using their newspapers much the way women would use fans.

"Yes! The late Lord Hampton...Had to carry him out of that woman's house. She didn't even care about him. I heard she was determined to keep the home. Messy business leaving that to the son to deal with. Even now that the family is out of their year of mourning, everyone hasn't forgotten old Hampton's sins." Caruthers sniffed pompously. "I wouldn't let my son be seen at dinner with that family, not with that sort of talk still hanging about."

"Indeed," the other man agreed. "Quite so—"

"Ahem," Leo growled softly as he stalked past the two men, his fists clenched in rage. Both of them jumped; apparently they'd deceived themselves into thinking he couldn't hear them. *Deaf old fools*. Even at his own bloody club, he couldn't escape the rumors, the whispering, the damned utter black scandal that his late father had brought down on his head. He didn't want to remember having to deal with his father's mistress or paying her off by letting her keep the house his father had purchased. The need to silence her and quiet the scandal as quickly as he could hadn't been as successful as he'd hoped. London ballrooms and dinners caught rumors and scandals, spreading them like wildfire.

Caruthers and his companion, now silent, watched him with keen interest as he settled in the only empty seat, one by the window facing St. James Street. On the street there was a mixture of motorcars and carriages. London was always busy in the fall with the season in full swing. For a brief moment, he let his thoughts wander away from the pain of listening to his family's private business be fodder for entertainment. If only he could get in his car and drive away from it all...

Despite the silence in the room, Leo knew that every man was focused on him.

He raked a hand through his blond hair and stifled a

groan. He'd been in London for all of three days, feverishly trying to secure investment opportunities and join in speculation schemes but it was no use. No one would work with him.

Father has damned me and Mother for his selfishness!

The spike of rage inside Leo was startling and so unlike him, but after having more than one door closed in his face today, he was exhausted. Even though it had been a year since his father had died, the scandal and the fervor behind it had yet to fade. His poor mother, Mina, refused to leave the countryside, knowing she'd have no real friends left in London who would allow her entrance to their homes. All because his father hadn't been faithful. It was an accepted albeit awful practice for a man to carry on an affair, but a man didn't die in his mistress's bed after a night of bed play, and he certainly didn't wrack up debts to pay for the care and keeping of that mistress. Yet that was exactly what his father had done.

Leo reached into his pocket and removed a letter that his footman had delivered to him before he'd left for the club. He opened it, smoothing out the paper and reading the hastily written lines from his banker, praying for much needed good news.

Lord Hampton,

It is with my deepest regret that we cannot extend any of your family's lines of credit at this time. We will be happy to discuss more credit if you can bring us new collateral but until then, the estate and all of your tenant farms connected thereto are fully mortgaged and cannot be further used to obtain additional credit.

Sincerely,

Thomas Atkinson

The words filled Leo's stomach with an empty ache. He had to find a way to stabilize his family's estate or he would risk losing his mansion in the country. Hampton House was his home, more so than London ever would be, and to think of creditors pawing at his family's furniture and running amok through the rooms of his childhood...

I won't let it happen. He would find someone to invest with, and he would bury his father's scandal in whatever way he could by living a life above society's reproach. He was going to marry a good English rose and not make the same mistakes his father did by allowing himself to become obsessed with some exotic beauty. Those sort of women were *always* trouble.

He had always believed he might marry someday for love and have a wife who was as passionate as he was, but those dreams were dashed now. He had chosen a neighboring viscount's daughter as his future bride for financial reasons. It was a chilling thought that he would soon tie his future to a woman without love, but it must be done.

"Hampton?" A familiar voice shook him from his dark thoughts. Striding toward him was a man he recognized.

"Hadley!" He grinned as relief at his friend's appearance swept through him. He got to his feet and shook Owen Hadley's hand. His dark-haired friend was smiling widely. Once, as boys at Eton, they had been inseparable, but then Owen and their friend Jack had gone off to fight in South Africa in the Second Boer War. When they returned, Jack and Owen had...changed. Leo hadn't been able to leave to go fight; his father hadn't allowed it. The estate was entailed to a male heir and as the only son, if Leo had perished beneath an African sun, some distant cousin would have taken over Hampton.

"Haven't seen you at the club in ages." Hadley sat across from him at the small table beside the window. It didn't escape Leo's notice that Hadley's clothes, while finely tailored, were a season out of fashion. Money troubles were apparently all the rage this season for young bachelors. Leo had enough money to pay his creditors now, but if he didn't find a way to produce new income soon, he would be in trouble.

"I've been in the country." Leo hastily tucked the banker's letter back into his coat pocket.

Owen's keen eyes missed little but he didn't ask what the letter was about. "You look tired, old friend."

"Do I?" Leo mused glumly. "Since my father died, it has been a trial to set the estate to rights."

"Are you afraid you'll lose it?" Owen asked quietly.

"No...at least not yet." Leo sighed. "But I cannot get a single man in London to let me partake in investments or speculation. The economy of the tenant farms simply isn't what it used to be and we need more stability." He leaned back in the leather armchair, wishing he could stay here in the club and not have to face the world outside.

"Cheer up!" Owen grinned. "Why don't we go find something to entertain us? It's been months and you could use some fun."

Leo shook his head. As much as he wished to throw his cares to the wind, he couldn't. His father's scandal had forced him to live a life of boredom. It was the only way he might find favor with society again, and that was crucial if he was to preserve Hampton House and everyone who depended on him.

"Perhaps another time. I suppose I ought to get back to Hampton at any rate. Lord knows what Mother will have gotten up to while I was away."

His friend laughed heartily. "Your mother is a dear. Any trouble she causes is a delight."

Leo brushed his hair back from his eyes. "You don't have to live with her."

"Touché." Owen shrugged. "At least she's not involved

with those suffragettes. You know they're having meetings all over the country right now?"

"Lord, don't even breathe a word of women's rights around my mother." Leo and Owen both glanced around the club to make sure no one was listening. Talking of suffragettes had a way of rousing trouble in a gentleman's club, one of the few places that completely barred women.

"Well, I won't keep you, Hampton, but write to me the next time you're in town. We should have a drink."

"Agreed." Leo shook Owen's hand and they both rose from their chairs. It would have been a fine thing to sit and talk with his old friend. They'd survived much together, but after today with his failures and knowing the talk of scandal was still clinging to his family even after a year, he was ready to run home with his tail tucked firmly between his legs. Tomorrow he would find another way to protect his home...tomorrow.

CHAPTER 2

"Now that your father is dead, I intend to indulge in scandalous behavior."

Leo choked on the sandwich he'd just bitten into. He'd been back from London for only one day, and his mother was already trying to kill him. His gaze shot to her face. The Dowager Countess of Hampton slid into a chair opposite him at the large oak dining room table where he was currently eating luncheon. She smoothed her lace tea gown over her lap and fixed him with a steady gaze.

Blood roared through his ears as he struggled to dislodge the bit of sandwich from his throat. *Damn cucumber...can't get it out...*He coughed violently and was finally able to get a bit of breath back in his lungs.

"Breathe, my dear, breathe," she intoned gently as though instructing a child of four, not her grown son of thirty-two. He adored his mother, but she had the uncanny ability of rankling him when he least needed to be rankled.

He reached forward and snatched his water goblet, hastily gulping the liquid. A cold nose nudged his other hand and he glanced down, seeing Ladybird, his chocolate-colored English cocker spaniel, lean against his knee. She whined softly when their eyes met. At least there was one sympathetic female in this house that wasn't determined to do him in.

"Mother," Leo finally got out. "What on earth are you talking about?" Could a man not enjoy a simple meal in peace? His eyes flicked heavenward as he prayed for patience. He supposed he should count himself lucky.

Before his father had died, he, Owen, and Jack had been constantly treading the line between propriety and scandal. He had caused more than one lady's father to eye him askance during a house party or a ball. Leo openly admitted he loved pleasure and the challenge of wooing a woman into his bed. But those days were gone. He was supposed to be keeping out of trouble to restore the family name. The last thing he needed was his mother getting into more trouble than usual.

The dowager countess perched regally, and one hand brushed a few loose hairs back into her elaborate coiffure. The light threading of silver amidst the gold was the only hint of her middling years having just passed. Considering how unhappy her marriage had been to his father, it was impressive that she still looked so well. It never ceased to upset him to think his father had spent nights in the arms of another when he had a beautiful wife at home. But then again, his father had been quite a fool.

"We are finally out of our year of mourning, and I wish to *enjoy* life." Her words were wistful in a way that made his chest tight. Her eyes narrowed as she continued. "I wasn't allowed to do so while the old tyrant still lived." The biting edge to her tone made him wince.

He had known his parents suffered through a loveless marriage, but her frankness about it was a little unsettling. One was not supposed to talk of such things so openly, but his mother had always been open. She was wild where his father had been cold and calm. He'd taken after her in that regard, and she'd never once challenged him on his rakish ways or his tendency to break the hearts of young ladies. But that was because he was a man; a lady had a higher duty to herself and to society to avoid scandal. If his mother was talking of living recklessly, he did not want to know the details. Leo dreaded whatever scheme she was planning now that she could enter society again without violating the strict dictates of her mourning period.

"Well?" She lifted a teacup to her lips, sipping it patiently.

"Well what?" He drank his water and studied her over the rim of the crystal glass. Since his father had died, he'd grown closer to his mother and he'd learned to read her. Right now, she was waiting for him to make the first move in this game she was playing.

For the last few months she'd been working tirelessly to get him away from Hampton House and to return to London. He knew he should be suspicious of her schemes but he wasn't going to fall back into old habits, no matter how tempting it would be to call upon his friends, spend nights at his club, live the life of a wild bachelor as he'd done well enough before his father died. Things were different now.

I cannot be that man anymore, the carefree fool who didn't know his life was on the brink of collapse.

His father's passing had left a hefty amount of death taxes that could bankrupt Hampton, and it was Leo's duty to find a way out from under that crushing weight. After the last three days in London and his continued failures to find a source of additional income, he was afraid for the future of his family. His estate wasn't the only one in danger of being broken by debts.

Only last week he'd visited the neighboring property to the west and learned that the Ashfords were selling their house because Lord Ashford's death had left them deeply in debt. An auctioneer had been examining family portraits and the collection of china and silver while Lady Ashford wept quietly in the corner of the drawing room, her two children sitting beside her, faces drawn tight with grief. It was a bloody bleak affair and Leo would not let that happen to Hampton. Even if it meant sacrificing his own happiness, he would see the estate remain intact.

His mother cleared her throat when he failed to respond. "Let's hear your objections. I know you wish to stop me and will insist we both live frugally and quietly."

Those very words had been on the tip of his tongue. He was a man of business and was keeping the Hampton estate alive based on such notions. Still...he preferred not to face his mother's obvious scorn over the valuable life lesson his father's passing had taught him. To care for a vast estate, a man could not simply gallivant about and live like a veritable rogue as he had when he'd been younger. It was even more important that he work to clear the Hampton name in society or they would be in dire straits before long. His father's mistress and the unsavory way he'd passed in her bed had set tongues wagging and doors slamming in his face so hard that Leo was afraid he might never be viewed reputably.

His days of wildness were behind him. He had his duty to his lands and to his family. They could not let this house be sold or their lives destroyed by losing a home that had been his family's for three hundred years.

"What"—he paused, hoping his concern didn't show—"exactly do you intend to do by indulging in scandalous behavior?" It was entirely possible that his mother's idea of scandal was far tamer than his. They were called the gentler sex for a reason.

"I am going into the village to attend a little political meeting. I've arranged to meet some ladies who share my views and—"

"Good God! You aren't talking about that women's suffrage nonsense, are you?" Leo set his napkin on the table and scowled imperiously at his mother.

Mina's brows arched and her spine stiffened. "I most certainly am. I am quite moved by their cause. Did you know we once had the right to vote? Back in the days of feudal society?"

Leo groaned and nearly smacked his palm into his forehead in frustration. God's teeth, this was not a matter he wished to be dealing with.

"Mother, you cannot go to any such meeting, and I don't give a bloody damn if women were voting back in the days of mud and squalor. That was the damned middle ages for Christ's sake. People were dropping dead of plague and nothing in life was certain. Now things are safe; there's no need for women to have a vote. The men of this country are quite capable of deciding matters of state for you."

The stark look of pain and rage in his mother's eyes was startling. He hadn't expected to see her react so...openly to his words.

"How can you say that...to *me*? After the way your father made us live, you would continue to deprive me of a voice?"

Leo rubbed his temples. "*No*, that's not what I meant, Mother. Please, try to understand. I have much to do and I cannot be worrying about you. People in London are talking..." He didn't want to continue but he had to make her understand that her actions could make matters worse.

"Talking? About what?" she asked quietly. Her blue eyes were dark and shadowed now.

"Father, about him and that woman. I couldn't get in to see half the gentlemen I used to before."

His mother seemed to understand now, her blue eyes wide with worry. "It's the money, isn't it? You're worried and we've lost so much face because of...*him*."

His throat tightened painfully and he nodded. He had let her down, had failed to do what he needed to in London, and it was destroying him to see her realize that.

She leaned over and placed one hand on top of his on the table, squeezing it. "Then I shan't go to the meeting. I would like a house party instead. Surely we can afford that?" she asked, hope brimming in her tone.

He smiled a little. "Yes, we can certainly afford a house party, Mother."

She brightened again, the worries chased quickly away. "Excellent! I wish to have it next weekend. Guests will arrive here on Friday and stay through Monday. I'm planning to invite all sorts of people, including Mr. Leighton. He owns the *London News Weekly*, which has all of those sensational articles regarding social and political intrigue. He has a lovely daughter—"

Ahh, therein lies her true goal. Not scandal, but marriage. He almost wondered if her plans to join the ranks of the suffragettes was merely to rile him up. No doubt she assumed he would agree to a house party instead because it was much less scandalous...and it would give her a chance to throw eligible ladies at his feet.

Leo's lips twitched. She was clever, his mother, but not clever enough to fool him into putting himself up for sale on the marriage mart. He waved a hand in the air.

"No. No matchmaking. You know full well that I intend to propose to Mildred Pepperwirth." He had been planning this for the last two months. He'd been to see their neighbors in Pepperwirth Vale and had made his intentions to Viscount Pepperwirth quite clear. Mildred was a good, solid choice for a wife. Beautiful, intelligent, and with a clean established English pedigree that would raise the Hampton title back up in the eyes of society.

An extremely unladylike snort escaped his mother's lips.

"Bah! Mildred Pepperwirth. Leo, dear, are you determined to give me dull, witless grandchildren? Don't repeat my mistakes." Her eyes darkened and the lines around her eyes and mouth seemed more pronounced as she frowned. "Marry for love. Marry a woman who makes you furious, who drives you mad, a woman who makes your heart bleed if you even think of living one day without her. Don't marry some simpering fool with a hefty dowry simply because you feel compelled to do your duty to your father and this house. She isn't the woman for you. You need someone forward thinking, dear, and Mildred...well...She is far too traditional."

"Traditional is exactly what I need, Mother. You'd have me marry some suffragette who'd tear down the laws and rules that keep our society intact? It would destroy my estate." How the devil had his mother circled back to the topic he wished for her to forget?

"I think those women who fight for the vote are wonderful!" His mother's voice rose a little and color deepened her cheeks. If he wasn't careful, he'd upset her again and he didn't want to do that. *Best to concede some battles in order to win the war, as Owen Hadley would say*. Owen would know, of course, seeing as how he'd fought in the war where battles had been all too real.

"They are indeed brave ladies, Mother. I wouldn't disagree on that. I simply think they would not make the most respectable of wives. I need someone I can depend upon to support my decisions for the estate, not undermine them." A woman with her head in the clouds, dreaming of voting and equal rights was...trouble. He could admire a woman for fighting for something she believed in, but he certainly didn't want to marry a woman like that.

"You'd doom yourself to a life without love?" Her voice trembled slightly as though she were deeply wounded by his reaction. She made as if to stand, but he reached out, caught her hand, and held it.

"Mother, sit. *Please.*" Her words stirred something in him, and he wasn't sure if he liked the idea...to get so lost in another person that you could not live without them. His father had done that with his mistress, a woman who hadn't cared for him the moment she knew her furnished lifestyle was at an end. Leo wanted to avoid such a fate with every fiber of his being.

Living a reckless bachelor life was one thing, but he'd never been foolish enough to allow himself to fall in love. It would be far too dangerous to open one's self up to such a weakness. He didn't want anyone to have power over his heart. His mother had loved his father, and she'd ended up perfectly unhappy when he'd abandoned her for a mistress. Love was a risk he would not take. He shoved the idea out of his mind, focusing on things he knew he could control.

"I think a house party is a wonderful idea, Mother. But do invite some people *I* know. I saw Hadley at the club yesterday. Drop him an invitation for me. In fact, invite the Pepperwirths as well." He winked at her. She rolled her eyes and sighed dramatically. He swore she muttered something about Mildred under her breath. Leo stifled a laugh. As long as his mother was in a mood to fence with him verbally, that meant she was all right and he hadn't upset her too terribly by refusing to let her attend the suffragette meeting.

He wasn't thrilled about the social obligations that houseguests would create, but he couldn't deny he had been burdened lately with far too much work. A party might improve his mood if only for the distraction it would provide. It was a pity he was no longer able to indulge in old habits. The Leo Graham he'd once been would have made it his mission to bed every willing and lovely lady under his roof.

Damn being respectable. It was going to kill him.

I'll have to find some other means of entertainment.

Keeping his mother from marrying him off to someone during the party would be his chief objective, and it would be amusing to see what schemes she came up with.

"You really insist I invite the Pepperwirths?"

He nodded, biting his lip to hide a smile as he enjoyed her squirming. He knew she liked Lord and Lady Pepperwirth, but she balked at his idea of marrying Mildred, simply because she found Mildred boring.

His mother threw up her hands and huffed. "Leo, shame on you. I expected more of a reaction than that. How is it you're a child of *my* blood?"

She stood to leave, and he could only sit back in his chair and glance down at Ladybird. Her canine brown eyes met his, and she seemed just as perplexed as he was by the entire situation. Her tail thumped the ground rhythmically and she nudged his hand until he stroked her head.

His mother wanted him to run off with a woman who made his blood burn. He couldn't afford to. Hampton needed its earl to be calm and in control. Many of his peers were not adjusting to the new age and thus were losing everything their families had built over centuries. His mother was too old-fashioned to see the changes sweeping England. Farmland was less valuable, and the tenancies on the estate weren't prospering as they had in the past.

Leo couldn't even begin to count the hours he'd spent working until the last candle burned out in his study. Or the endless meetings he'd arranged with his steward, Mr. Holmesbury, as they tried to salvage what they could of a crumbling way of life. *Their way of life.* Everything that mattered to him. They could lose it all if he didn't succeed. Grand houses cost far too much, as did the servants they employed.

Running the tip of his finger over the white china plates fringed with a blue flower pattern, he drew in a deep breath.

A heavy weight settled over his chest and shoulders, an invisible burden he could not remove, not so long as he continued to love Hampton House and the people who lived within it. They were a part of this place, a part of its history, just as he was.

If any sacrifices could be made, he would fight to keep Hampton just as it was for as long as possible. He had made his plans. He would marry Mildred, use her fortune to sustain Hampton during the transitions taking place in England, and that would be the end of it. Nothing would change his mind. *Nothing.*

❧

Wilhelmina, Dowager Countess of Hampton, peered around the door to the dining room, watching her son finish his luncheon in silence. Ever since he'd returned from London a week ago, he'd been glum and predictable in his daily routine. Working from morning till midnight.

Leo took another bite of his lunch before he reached for the stack of letters on the silver tray to his left, a soft sigh escaping as his shoulders drooped. Ladybird sat at his side, tail swiping across the floor in gentle swishes as she waited for crumbs. The dog whined softly and he petted her absently.

He painted a perfectly boring picture of country life, and it deepened the ache in her heart for him. Leo had been a wonderful child, always exploring, always questing for adventures and causing trouble, the way any good lad should. Mina hadn't been deaf to the rumors of his many paramours or the broken hearts he'd left behind him. At least he'd been a man of passion and action.

Now he was...not. This new Leo was not a son she wished to call her own. He was world-weary, his eyes dark with sorrow and his lips perpetually pursed as he let worries and anxieties drown him. How could he not see that only the bold and courageous men would continue on in this new world, where the ancient houses were crumbling and being broken apart?

She shuddered. The Ashfords had heard their home would be gutted and the grand staircases, the tapestries, even the marble tiles would be sold off to different bidders. Nothing would be left of the grand house or the family who had lived there nearly as long as the Grahams had lived at Hampton House.

We are soon to be ghosts of a forgotten era. We must change; we must adapt. It was one of the reasons she was so determined to attend the suffragette meeting in the small village close to Hampton House. A good number of ladies were coming down from London to attend in order to escape the harsh reactions their gathering would draw in London. Things had to change; *people* had to change. Men needed to recognize that women were just as smart and as valuable in society.

Leo could not marry a traditional woman. He needed someone who would stand at his side and face the future without fear. Mina would do just about anything to see him married to a fierce Amazon who would battle at his side.

"My lady?" Mr. Gordon, the butler, whispered as he joined his mistress by the door.

She turned and placed a finger to her lips and pointed to Leo.

"Have all the preparations been made for our guests?"

Gordon's face, usually a study of seriousness, softened with pride, and he puffed his chest a bit. "Of course, my lady. I received a telegram from Mr. Leighton. Miss Ivy is coming down early in her father's motorcar."

Mina moved back a few steps from the door as she clapped her hands together in silent glee. Her plan was coming together perfectly. She'd invited Ivy down to Hampton on the pretext of attending the suffragette meeting together, and she'd convinced the young lady that visiting for the house party would be fun.

"Did Mr. Leighton say if he was able to tamper with the motorcar?"

Gordon frowned a little, concern darkening his expression as he handed her the folded telegram. He had known Miss Ivy as long as Mina had and the idea of putting her at risk seemed to upset him.

"Mr. Leighton assured me her motorcar would be close enough to the house but that she'd be stranded. We should make sure to suggest his lordship take a drive around half-past two on Friday. He'll be sure to come across her on the main road."

She hastily read the note herself, grinning a little before slipping it into her dress pocket.

Poor Leo. He was most determined to marry that awful Pepperwirth girl. If all went according to Mina's plans, his intended betrothal would soon be at an end, and her son would fall in love with a woman far more worthy of him. A girl he'd known many years ago, one who'd loved him with all her heart before tragedy had forced their destinies apart.

Ivy Leighton was a modern woman who shared Mina's views on women's rights and would be the best match for her son. Assuming he could see past the fact that she was a suffragette. Mina's lips twitched. No doubt when he met Ivy again, he would find her very grown up and very much changed from the little girl who used to stare at him with stars in her eyes and her heart on her sleeve. She only hoped he would see Ivy as Mina did, as the woman who could save his soul and save Hampton House.

Perhaps I am a meddlesome mama, but Leo should know that I won't leave his choice of wife up to fate.

CHAPTER 3

Ivy Leighton swiped at the billowing black clouds smothering her. Coughing, she removed her driving goggles and tossed them onto the seat of her new Hudson Speedabout. The *broken* speedabout. Her father was going to be furious. She'd asked to drive it, and only a few miles from her destination, the engine had made a ghastly screeching sound like a dying falcon. Dark smoke plumed out from beneath the yellow hood, painting a dark picture against the deep blue sky.

"Oh dear," she groaned.

She wiped her brow with the back of a gloved hand and it came away dirty. A cool September breeze teased at a loose tendril of her hair from beneath her flat hat. She tried to brush it away, but the thick veil tied around her hat made it more than a little complicated. She unbuttoned her tan linen duster, feeling a little flustered by the Hudson's sudden failure.

What on earth was she going to do? Walk to Hampton House? Why had she thought coming early by herself was a good idea? Because she was plagued by curiosity. Sixteen years ago she had left Hampton, her mother's body barely cold in the ground. How much had the place changed? How much had *he* changed?

Leo...his name still made her shiver.

Handsome, charming Leo. When she'd been eight, he'd been sixteen, and a lifetime seemed to have separated them. Now she was twenty-four and he had to be...she did the math. Thirty-two? Would he still have the ability to consume her soul with those fathomless blue eyes? A part of her was afraid to see him again after all these years. Had her girlhood memories been the stuff of fantasies or was he still the man she'd always loved?

After six Seasons in London, she hadn't found anyone who measured up to Leo Graham, the Earl of Hampton, and she feared she never would. But...what if she arrived at Hampton House and found that he wasn't the man she believed him to be?

With a little shake of her head, Ivy recalled the way he used to tease her, tap the tip of her nose with a finger and call her Button.

"Button indeed," she muttered.

Her nose was no longer buttonlike, at least not completely. Leo hadn't seen her since she'd outgrown her oversized eyes, knobby knees, and pert nose. Ivy tried to quell the fleet of butterflies that stormed against the battlements of her stomach.

She was nothing like the English beauties who were so favored by the gentlemen at the balls during the Season. That was the problem with being half Gypsy rather than a full-blooded English rose. Still, she knew she was pretty, in an exotic sort of way, but would Leo think her desirable? Ivy had been a favorite of many men. Her father's position, as well as her own heritage, made them believe she had no morals.

A non-Romani or *gadjo's* sense of Gypsies was always

wrong. Women of the Romani culture were anything but loose. Still, that awful cultural misunderstanding led to more than one man to offer her a position as his mistress. An offer that she had to politely refuse without making a scene, even though such a request deserved a slap.

Hopefully Leo would be different.

Not that I should truly care, she reminded herself. She was only coming to Hampton House to see the dowager countess and to attend a suffragette meeting with her. Lady Hampton had insisted that Ivy stay for the house party. She'd reminded Leo's mother that she wasn't coming to husband hunt but to see old friends. Ivy firmly believed a modern woman couldn't have a husband, at least not a man born into the British peerage. They stood against women's rights and that was something that she could never reconcile.

She'd watched her mother work tirelessly as a servant for years in a world where her voice hadn't mattered. Witnessing her mother's inability to live the life she truly wanted before she'd died had changed Ivy. Without the right and the power to speak, a person ceased to exist.

After her mother died, she'd been reunited with her father and it had become clear just how powerless she was as a woman. Although he loved and adored her, even he could not give her power over her own life in the way men had. She could not even control her own inheritance; it had to be held in trust by a man. It seemed like everywhere she turned was a dead end. No way out. To be ensnared in a gilded cage meant she was still trapped. The thought made her recoil. Marry a man who would trap her and destroy her independence? No, she would never agree to that. But still...seeing Leo again after all this time would be nice.

Turning her attention back to the Hudson, she knew she'd have to leave it on the shoulder of the road for now. As she reached for her valise, the gravel on the road slipped beneath her boots. A panicked cry escaped her lips as she fell headfirst into the space behind the driver's seat. Her legs wiggled in the air as she struggled in vain to propel herself back upright.

"Blast and hell!" she cursed, fighting wildly to get her body into a position that could leverage her back down. Her dress and coat tangled around her knees.

The purr of another motorcar's engine made her freeze. A cool breeze caressed her where her travel dress bunched around her thighs. Whoever had just stopped on the road had a prime view of her legs.

The motor died. Footsteps crunching on gravel warned her of someone's approach, and her body went rigid in apprehension. Fear ratcheted up inside her until she was gasping for breath and thrashing to get back on her feet.

"Er...excuse me, miss. May I help?" a rich, smooth voice asked.

"Oh, yes, please. I'm in a spot of bother it seems."

"I'm going to touch you, miss. Please do not panic." The man's gloved hands settled on her ankles, then slid to her calves as he pulled her down. Tingles of awareness shot through her body, making her twitch in the oddest places.

Ivy tried not to let it ruffle her that some strange man's hands were on her legs. She'd never liked feeling vulnerable, and this was perhaps the most exposed she'd ever been in her life. It was unsettling to say the least. She slid down the side of the Hudson, her face heating and the blood pounding in her ears. When she turned to her rescuer, her heart skittered to a stop, and she sucked in a breath.

Leo.

For a long moment she couldn't think, couldn't breathe. She was a girl again, crying as her mother lay dying. Leo's long, muscular body had been solid and warm behind her as he held her while she wept. He'd been comfort and heat and light where she'd only endured darkness in her mother's last hours.

Of course it would be *him*. He'd be the one to find her covered in road dust, legs flailing in the air, and stuck with a broken down motorcar. She was always at her worst when he was around. Lady Fate evidently didn't like her.

Is there no end to my bad luck?

"Thank you," she said, uncertain if she should say her name. Would he even remember her? Surely not...

With an unexpected deftness, he adjusted her hat, which had been knocked slightly askew during her tumble into the motorcar, and pushed the sides of the veil back as though to get a better look at her face. His lips kicked into a grin, and her heart fluttered back to life. Lord, the man was handsome. His aquiline nose and strong jaw, lips a little thin, but no less appealing, and a halo of golden hair blowing in the breeze. And those eyes, eyes she'd dreamt about for years. More beautiful than she'd remembered.

"You're welcome, Miss..." He waited for her to introduce herself.

So he didn't remember her, then? It stung, yet perhaps that was for the best, given the secret mission Leo's mother had entrusted her with. It was best he did not recognize her and she did not wish to be remembered as "Button."

"My name is Ivy Leighton."

Her name had no effect on him, not that it should have. She'd taken her father's surname after she'd left Hampton and she couldn't remember a time when Leo had called her Ivy. Perhaps he didn't even know it was her name. She hadn't mentioned her mother's maiden name, Jameson, so there was the real possibility he wouldn't recognize her at all. Ivy wasn't a unique name, not really.

Leo captured one of her gloved hands and pressed a kiss to her knuckles. "It's a pleasure to meet you, Miss Leighton, even under such trying circumstances." His lips twitched at the last few words as though he was doing his best not to tease her. "I see you are having some difficulties with your automobile." His eyes roved over the state of the smoking motorcar behind her, assessing the situation.

She tilted her head to the side. Something was different about him, and it wasn't simply that he'd grown into a man and left the last traces of his boyhood behind. No...he had changed, and she couldn't put her finger on how. There was a seriousness to him, a grave solemnity of a man who'd suffered tragedy and loss and now bore a heavy burden. It gave her a bittersweet longing for the young man he'd once been and a respect for the man he'd become now. One thing that had not changed was the effect of his devastating smile. He could have made a fortune bottling it and selling it to lonely hearts throughout England.

In his unbuttoned Burberry motoring coat, trousers, and cap, Leo looked every inch a man of leisure. Yet a silver pocket watch chain glinting in the sunlight lent him an air of authority and precision. An altogether different impression from the boy he'd once been who'd spent an evening capturing glow worms with her in the garden or comforting her after she'd had a rough day and scraped her knee while running about.

She remembered grinning at him so broadly her cheeks hurt as he bent down to show her a captured insect between his palms. The green light had illuminated his face as he studied the black insect. In that moment, they'd been bound together by a spell of twilight and an effervescent glow. Having to stay still, breaths held, so as not to frighten the shy glowworm into darkening her shine. Her heart clenched in longing for warm summer nights like those again. She swallowed the sudden sense of homesickness for a place she'd forced herself to try and forget.

"It was very kind of you to stop and help a lady in distress." She offered a smile, hoping the action would lift her spirits. She had to put memories of that sixteen-year-old boy with merry, twinkling eyes and a tempting smile behind her or she'd be lost. *He's not for you; you cannot fall in love with him, not again.* The Leo she faced now was businesslike and polite, with only a hint of that charming, troublemaking boy she remembered so well.

What had changed him? Had his mother been right that his father's death and the pressures of running the estate had turned him cool and passionless? She'd heard some of the rumors about his father but wasn't sure if they were true. Given how the whispers of his father's mistress had persisted, it had likely affected his reception with most of the respectable families in the city. Even now she could see a hint of that resigned expression in his beautiful eyes. Where was the fiery young man who'd stolen her heart? *No wonder Lady Hampton begged me to come visit him.*

"I'm sorry, I haven't introduced myself. I am the Earl of Hampton. I would be delighted to help, though I confess to knowing nothing of motorcar engines. If you permit, I shall escort you to your destination and send my mechanic to repair your automobile and return it to you." As Leo spoke, he leaned in, placing one hand against the car beside her hip, and she shivered at the scent of him and his warmth. She had always been aware of him; like a planet hugging a distant star, she was connected to him in ways she'd never been with any other man. And that was what made him so dangerous to her. He was perhaps the one man in all of England who could tempt her into falling in love. And love would ruin all of her dreams for a brighter future as a woman with rights. Still, she had promised Lady Hampton she would visit the house and see Leo; she simply needed to guard her heart while she was here.

"My lord, it seems we are both fortunate. My destination is in fact Hampton House. I was invited by the countess for her house party."

This caught him by surprise. His eyes narrowed slightly as his gaze swept her body. Within her tan duster covered in dirt, Ivy must have looked a fright. Not that she could have helped her appearance, but she would have loved to have met him again under better circumstances.

Comprehension showed in the widening of his eyes as he made some mental connection. "My mother invited you? You aren't the newspaper fellow's daughter, are you?"

The newspaper fellow? So Lady Hampton had mentioned her coming, then. Over tea, Lady Hampton had outlined a scheme to play a game upon Leo that required some level of discretion as to Ivy's identity. Leo's mother was convinced he would be too well behaved if he realized Ivy had once been the child he'd looked after. It would be better to hide her identity for a time so she could be treated like any other lady he might meet. The idea of deception hadn't set well with Ivy, but she had to admit she did not want him thinking of Button during the house party.

I'll tell him who I really am, after he has a chance to know me as a woman.

"My father is indeed the newspaperman." She chuckled. He wasn't the first to react that way to her father's background. Leo's eyes were still fixed upon her face and she tried not to wriggle under the intense scrutiny of his gaze. It made her feel warm in the oddest places, and it was much more like the Leo she'd known as a girl.

"Fortunate indeed that I found you, then." He looked over her shoulder into the motorcar. "Your luggage?"

Before she could step out of the way, he moved, accidentally pressing her against the door. A flush of heat coursed through her in a sudden rush when he didn't immediately step back. His eyes blazed with an unexpected interest that made her feel small and vulnerable. As though he could see through her, pick apart her soul, and study the pieces and understand her. What a terrifying thought...Never had she wanted a man to evoke such a feeling, but with him, it was exciting, rather than frightening. Ivy licked her lips and his eyes tracked the movements the way a lion would a mouse.

"Your"—he breathed deeply—"bag," he murmured, sliding past her to reach into the Hudson. He retrieved it without any of the trouble she'd had. "This way."

He gestured toward his auto, which was parked next to hers.

It was a lovely black Stanley Touring motorcar. Her father had almost bought the same model instead of the Hudson, but in the end he'd opted for the striking yellow auto, valuing the flash more than the extra seats.

Leo walked ahead of her, placing her luggage behind the front passenger seat.

Ivy retrieved her eye goggles and hastily got into her side of the Stanley, which earned her a raised brow by Leo, who had only just turned to try and open the door for her. For some reason, she needed a moment of space between them, at least long enough to get her breath and her good sense back. How was a woman supposed to concentrate around such an irresistible man? When he was too close, she seemed to think only of him and wonder if his lips were as soft as they looked.

Once they were driving back down the road, he turned to look at her.

"Are you traveling alone? Mother mentioned your father was coming. I'm sure she would have insisted you be escorted." There was a note of disapproval to his voice that she didn't like.

She hesitated before replying. "My father is coming

tomorrow afternoon on the train, and he's bringing my lady's maid and his valet. Your mother said one of her upstairs maids could wait upon me until they arrived."

"So was that your father's Hudson?"

The question prickled her because his tone seemed to imply a woman could not own a motorcar. It was her father's but only because she insisted they share a vehicle, when he offered to buy her one of her own. They didn't need two; that would have been silly.

"It is," she replied a tad stiffly. "But I have plenty of experience driving it."

Let him think what he will about that.

Leo was silent for a moment. "So...you are...friends with my mother?"

Ivy nibbled her bottom lip, considering how best to answer that. Lady Hampton had always looked out for her as a child, especially when her mother fell ill. The countess was the one who had located Ivy's father and informed him that he had a daughter. For such a service, the word *friend* hardly seemed adequate. Leo's mother was a veritable godsend. But she was supposed to remember the little prank they were to play upon Leo by keeping her real name a secret for a time.

"We met in London three months ago at a charity function held by Lady Buxton." A lie. The countess had crafted a story to explain how they met to keep Leo from discovering Ivy's true identity. She also didn't want Leo knowing that she and Ivy were involved in the Women's Social and Political Union together. When Ivy had questioned the deceptive plan, Lady Hampton had explained her predicament vaguely, saying Leo had become too rigid, too driven, and wasn't open in his thinking, especially toward the suffragette movement.

"He needs adventure and mystery, my dear, and you can provide both. It shall be a fun game. He needs to be shocked for his own good."

But Ivy had grown up at Hampton House and worried the

servants would recognize her. The countess had insisted that the servants who'd known her as a child had been instructed to treat her as they would any guest, not as the child they had helped raise.

Ivy had no desire for "Button" to be resurrected in Leo's mind, and a few days of simply being herself would be fun. She would not play the deceiver long, though. She would tell Leo who she was soon; she would simply leave out his mother's involvement in the local suffragette gathering.

Lost in thought, she didn't immediately realize she was being a poor companion to him. A lady of good breeding would never let herself get lost in thought in the presence of her future host. She glanced at Leo and discovered he was watching her when not checking the road ahead.

"And your father? How did he meet my mother?"

"At the same event. She seemed to enjoy discussing his paper."

Leo's bark of laughter made her frown. "The newspaperman. Mother mentioned he was coming and is quite looking forward to it."

She hoped her father had the good sense to follow the instructions Lady Hampton gave him and not betray Ivy's true identity by mentioning her mother and Ivy's past at Hampton.

Ivy shivered, now feeling the chill in the air, and rubbed her arms.

"There's a lap rug beneath the seat." His hand bumped into hers as they both reached for it.

"My apologies," he murmured, and withdrew his hand. Ivy's gloved fingers brushed over the blanket. She hastily arranged it over her lap and legs, feeling instantly warmer.

"Thank you, my lord."

He merely nodded. The Stanley rattled and bounced worse than a coach on the road. After a few minutes, Leo spun the wheel and turned onto a gravel drive that stretched toward a massive manor house in the distance.

Hampton.

The vision of it always stole her breath. The tan stones were warm in the September sun and afternoon light glinted off the windowpanes. Fir trees dotted the open grounds in patches like spikes of deep green paint across a lighter emerald canvas. She had forgotten how vast the house was and how beautiful.

Nature blended with the house and the gardens, making it a private world where anything seemed possible. Memories of early morning mists curling around the grounds like milky tendrils stirred within her. She used to chase the peacocks across the lawn with Old John, Leo's old butterscotch-colored cocker spaniel, the dog nipping at the thousand-eyed plumed tail feathers of the ill-tempered birds. Old John had always been called that for as long as she could remember. Had he ever been Young John? She hadn't thought to ask. The silliness of her thoughts made her smile. Hampton had a way of reminding her of being a child again, in small ways that made her heart tighten in her chest. Like dancing rainbows in the library caught from a spinning diamond chandelier, or digging in the cool soil to plant seeds with the ancient gardener, Mr. Matthews.

A little sigh escaped Ivy as she thought of all the hours she'd spent there, the minutes ticking away, never knowing her mother would soon die and she'd lose part of herself forever. Or that she'd lose Hampton forever. Yet here she was, sitting in an automobile with Leo, *coming home*.

ABOUT THE AUTHOR

Lauren Smith is an Oklahoma attorney by day, author by night who pens adventurous and edgy romance stories by the light of her smart phone flashlight app. She knew she was destined to be a romance writer when she attempted to re-write the entire *Titanic* movie just to save Jack from drowning. Connecting with readers by writing emotionally moving, realistic and sexy romances no matter what time period is her passion. She's won multiple awards in several romance subgenres including: New England Reader's Choice Awards, Greater Detroit BookSeller's Best Awards, and a Semi-Finalist award for the Mary Wollstonecraft Shelley Award.

To Connect with Lauren, visit her at:
www.laurensmithbooks.com
lauren@laurensmithbooks.com

CPSIA information can be obtained
at www.ICGtesting.com
Printed in the USA
BVHW051948140622
639735BV00008B/884

9 781947 206427